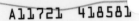

JO and the Bandit

JO and the Bandit

Willo Davis Roberts

A Jean Karl book

Atheneum   1992   New York

Maxwell Macmillan Canada
Toronto

Maxwell Macmillan International
New York   Oxford   Singapore   Sydney

Atheneum
Macmillan Publishing Company
866 Third Avenue
New York, NY 10022

Maxwell Macmillan Canada, Inc.
1200 Eglinton Avenue East
Suite 200
Don Mills, Ontario M3C 3N1

Macmillan Publishing Company is part of
the Maxwell Communication Group of Companies.

First edition
Printed in the United States of America
Designed by Eliza Green

10   9   8   7   6   5   4   3   2   1

The text of this book is set in 12/15 Caslon Old Face #2

Library of Congress Cataloging-in-Publication Data
Roberts, Willo Davis.
Jo and the bandit/Willo Davis Roberts.—1st ed.
p.   cm.
"A Jean Karl book."
Summary: En route to stay with her uncle in Texas in the late 1860s,
twelve-year-old Jo experiences a stagecoach robbery and becomes
involved with a reluctant young outlaw aiming to change his ways.
ISBN 0–689–31745–X
[1. Robbers and outlaws—Fiction.   2. Texas—Fiction.   3. West
(U.S.)—Fiction.]   I. Title.
PZ7.R54465Jo   1992
[Fic]—dc20   91–4100

To my granddaughter, Nicki

1

Josephine Eleanor Elizabeth Whitman winced as the stage-coach dropped a wheel into a hole and lurched out of it again, throwing her against her little brother so that Andrew let out a yelp.

"Sorry," Jo muttered, and wished she could get out of the seat for even a minute. They had been riding for the better part of four days, and her bottom ached from the hard boards beneath her.

Andrew sighed audibly. "I always wanted to ride a stage-coach, but I didn't mean to do it for the rest of my life. Do you think we'll be stopping pretty soon?"

"Not until we get to Muddy Wells," Mrs. Hilson said. She was an enormously fat woman, and she took up fully half of the seat, so that Jo and Andrew were squeezed together in the other half. It didn't seem quite fair, since they had each paid the same amount as Mrs. Hilson but were getting far less space to sit in. Yet it seemed better than being on the *other* seat. On that side, riding backward, were Mr. Doane, Mr. Levinger, and Mr. Shaker. They were just as crushed together, and besides that could only see where they'd been, not where they were going.

Mrs. Hilson had announced quite firmly, before they had even boarded the stage at the last stop, that if she had to ride backward she would surely be sick. "Always throw up, every time," she assured her fellow passengers, and the men grudgingly allowed her to choose her own seat, facing forward.

Mr. Doane was the undertaker in Muddy Wells. He had gone up to Dallas on unspecified business, and was on his way home. He was rather stout, though his stomach protruded to the front rather than to the sides. That was a good thing because Mr. Shaker, though he was what Grandma would have called a bean pole, had wide shoulders and needed all the space for them that he could get.

Andrew had been fascinated with Mr. Shaker from the moment he saw him. Jo had finally realized why when, as they pitched into and out of one of the uncountable potholes that marked the stage road, Mr. Shaker's coat flopped open for a moment. The man was wearing the silver badge of a deputy sheriff pinned to his shirt.

Andrew's curiosity could not be contained for long. He soon leaned forward and asked abruptly, "Are you a Texas Ranger, sir?"

The man lifted a thumb to push back the brim of his Stetson. "Nope. Just a deputy, when I'm not being a farmer."

Andrew squirmed forward. "Do you have a gun?"

The deputy pulled back his coat again, this time far enough so that he poked an elbow into the undertaker's paunch. "Wouldn't be much use without one," he said, revealing his holster and the weapon he carried there.

"Did you ever shoot anybody?" Andrew asked eagerly.

"Thirty-seven men, so far," Mr. Shaker asserted. And then, as an afterthought, he added, "And one woman."

Andrew's mouth sagged open. "Really?"

"Really."

Andrew moistened his lips. "Did you kill them all?"

"Nope. Only the ones I intended to kill. Seven of them. Took the others to jail."

At that point Jo was curious too. "Did you kill the woman?"

"Nope. Didn't intend to. Just didn't want *her* to kill *me*."

"Was she trying to?" Andrew asked. When he leaned forward that way, he gave Jo just a little more space for a few moments.

Mrs. Hilson oozed over into the extra space, and Jo struggled to hold her share.

The deputy let his coat fall back over his gun. "She surely was," he said in response to Andrew's question. "I had just handcuffed her baby boy and threw him over the back of a mule to haul him off to jail. She come out of the house with a rifle and drew a bead on me, and I plugged her in the shoulder. Put an end to that nonsense."

"Did you arrest her too?" Andrew might not be quite as impressed with Mr. Shaker as if he'd been a Texas Ranger, but a deputy sheriff was the next best thing.

"Nope. No need. She only wanted to protect her son, and with a hole through her shoulder she wasn't dangerous to nobody else."

"What had her son done?" Jo asked, pushing back against Mrs. Hilson for all she was worth and pulling Andrew back in beside her before he was ejected onto the floor of the coach.

"Robbed a bank, shot the teller. Old Judge Macklin had him strung up the day after I brought him in."

Jo swallowed. "Hanged, you mean?"

"That's right."

Andrew swallowed too, loudly enough so that Jo heard him over the thunder of the horses' hooves and the creaking of the coach. "He's our uncle," he said.

Mr. Shaker looked startled. "The bank robber? Billy Swamish?"

"No, Judge Macklin. We're going to live with him."

Jo was immediately aware of the attention of all the other passengers. Mrs. Hilson twisted about to stare at them more directly. "He know you're coming, does he, missy?"

She sounded so incredulous that Jo felt an uneasy sensation in the pit of her stomach. "Yes, of course. Sheriff Stanton wrote to him after Grandma died."

"Well," Mrs. Hilson said after a moment, "that ought to be interesting."

The undertaker, Mr. Doane, cleared his throat. Mr. Shaker nodded. "Sure will be," he agreed, and Jo's uneasiness grew, but she didn't quite dare ask why her fellow passengers thought their arrival might be unduly interesting.

At that very moment the coach pitched them all about so violently that by the time they'd sorted themselves out the topic was forgotten.

The remaining passenger, Mr. Levinger, had painfully smashed an elbow during the upset and spewed out a string of profanity that brought a sharp rebuke from the mortician, Mr. Doane. "There are ladies and children present, sir. Kindly restrain yourself."

Jo wondered if she was one of the children or one of the ladies. She was, after all, twelve years old and tall for her age, though she hadn't yet put her hair up.

Mr. Levinger apologized halfheartedly, his eyes watering as he rubbed the injured place. In a no-less furious voice, he issued a blistering indictment of the stagecoach, the driver, the road, and of Texas in general.

"Barbaric place," he concluded before he clamped his teeth together.

Mr. Levinger, a middle-aged gentleman in a bowler hat, came from Boston, which was evidently a very respectable and proper city. Boston was, in every way and according to Mr. Levinger, far superior to any part of Texas.

At first the other passengers had listened with interest to him tell about Boston. But after a time even Andrew grew tired of hearing how savage and untamed Texas was, and how everything in Boston, Massachusetts, was so much better.

Jo would have had to admit that the area they were traveling through now was not especially beautiful or exciting. Not the way it was in the Piney Woods where she had grown up. Jo loved the woods and the hills around Huntsville, especially in the spring when the bluebonnets and Indian paintbrushes and primroses made bright patches of color in the grass, and dogwood dappled the pale green leaves of the elm and oak trees with creamy splotches. She wished Mr. Levinger could see the Piney Woods country before he condemned all of Texas.

Jo stopped listening to Mr. Levinger's caustic comments and looked out the window. The land was flat and virtually featureless, with no wildflowers, only dirt and dry grass. And instead of forests of loblolly pines and elms to cast cooling shade, there were only a few cottonwoods along the occasional creek bed.

For a moment Jo's throat closed as a wave of homesickness swept over her. The longing to be back in Grandma's snug little house was so strong that her eyes stung.

Of course she *would* be going back to Huntsville and

the Piney Woods when Aunt Harriet arrived, but Grandma wouldn't be there. Grandma was buried beneath the wooden cross out on the hill beside Mama and Jo's little sister, Cecelia, who had died the year before Andrew was born.

Jo had never seen Pa's grave. It was a long way off, in Mississippi, where he had died in a skirmish with the Union forces, not even in one of the major battles. Jo had been only eight years old then.

She watched the Texas flatlands sliding by the stage window and wondered why life had to be so sad. Everybody she loved in the whole world, except for Andrew, was buried on some lonely hillside.

Aunt Harriet was Mama's sister, but Jo had never seen her. A long time ago, even before Mama and Pa got married, Aunt Harriet had married Uncle Travis and moved to Galveston, down on the Gulf of Mexico. She used to write letters to Mama sometimes, and Mama would laugh and cry over them, and read them over and over again.

So they didn't know Aunt Harriet, but she was going to raise them now until they were grown. It made Jo feel very strange, almost sick to her stomach, to think about being raised by a stranger. Of course she was nearly raised already, and no doubt in just a few years she'd meet some nice young man and get married. But Andrew was only nine, and he had a lot of growing up to do yet.

Grandma and Aunt Harriet had had a falling-out many years ago, and Grandma hadn't talked about her the way she did about Mama or even Uncle Matthew, so they didn't really know what Aunt Harriet was like. Nothing like Mama, Grandma had once said sourly. Whatever that meant. Anyway, Aunt Harriet was the only living relative they had, except for Uncle Matthew.

Uncle Matthew was Judge Macklin, who had caused Mrs. Swamish's baby boy to be hanged after Deputy Shaker had brought him in on the back of a mule. She supposed he hadn't really been a baby boy, only the youngest of Mrs. Swamish's children.

They'd never met Uncle Matthew, either, and Jo was no more sure of a welcome from the judge than she was from Aunt Harriet. Apparently the two of *them* had been feuding for years too. "Don't give up our grudges easy," Grandma always said of the family, and Jo guessed it was true, though Jo didn't see the sense of it herself. She sided more with Mama, who thought forgiving and forgetting was the better way. At least Jo felt one ought to forgive, though sometimes it must be nearly impossible to actually forget. She and Mama had talked about that once, and Mama had explained that in this case forgetting really meant just not going on about a person's shortcomings once you'd forgiven them.

She had a nasty suspicion she wasn't going to like either one of her remaining relatives, though every day she prayed she was wrong about that.

So far her prayers didn't seem to have done much good, she reflected, but maybe this time it would be different.

Beside her, Andrew sighed heavily. "I'll be glad when we get there," he said. "I'm sure tired of riding. Anything's going to be better than this."

Jo wasn't sure about that, either. Muddy Wells didn't sound like the Garden of Eden, exactly. All they knew about it was its name, which wasn't promising.

If all went the way it was supposed to, they wouldn't have to stay in Muddy Wells very long. As soon as Aunt Harriet had her new baby and got well enough to travel, she had promised to send for them. She was recently widowed, and she had decided that after Uncle Travis was drowned during a hurricane she didn't want to live along the coast anymore.

So, she had written, she would come and live in Grandma's house in the Piney Woods as soon as she was able to dispose of her property near Galveston. There weren't many people who could afford to buy land these days, not after the long war, which had left almost everyone in poverty, Aunt Harriet had written, so there was no telling how long it would take to find a buyer. But as soon as she could manage it, she would head for Huntsville and Grandma's house.

When their neighbor, Mrs. Jones, read that, she had been astonished. "Got a couple of young 'uns, ain't she?"

"Two boys and a new baby coming," Jo confirmed.

Mrs. Jones looked around the kitchen that also served as the parlor. "How on earth's she going to fit 'em all in?" she wondered aloud.

Jo wondered that too, but there were so many other things to worry about she didn't have time to waste worrying about that.

"We'll get along all right until she gets here," Jo said. "We have the garden in, and we can butcher the pig—"

Mrs. Jones gave her a strange look. "You're not figuring on staying here alone, just you and Andrew, are you, child?"

Jo was startled. "Why, I'd thought to, yes, ma'am."

"Oh, I shouldn't think your grandma would want that, girl."

Jo moistened her lips and swallowed before she could speak. "Why not? We have plenty to eat—chickens, and the cow—"

Mrs. Jones's mouth tightened. "You're only a couple of children. And this here farm is too isolated. You wouldn't be safe here by yourselves."

Not safe? Jo had lived here all her life, and had always felt as safe as anyone could be, though the wandering, homeless soldiers after the war had sometimes been momentarily frightening when they appeared. Grandma had usually given them a few chores to do—chopping wood was her favorite one—and given them a meal in return. She hadn't encouraged them to hang around, though, and on one occasion had firmly ordered a pair off the place. When they seemed reluctant to leave, she had picked up the old rifle and pointed it right at them. "Git," she said, and after only a moment's hesitation, they left.

Still, Jo hadn't felt in any particular danger then. She didn't really feel endangered now. "We'll be all right," she assured her neighbor.

"There's still those wandering around with no jobs, no homes," Mrs. Jones pointed out. "Looking to help themselves to whatever someone else has. They spent years fighting the Yankees, getting by with guns, not common sense. Some of 'em got in the habit of just taking what they want rather than working for it. No, child, it wouldn't be safe here, just the two of you. I'd take you in until your aunty gets here, but I plain don't have the space. Andrew's too little to sleep alone in the barn, and I wouldn't put a young *girl* out there, either. Never know when some tramp is going to choose your barn to sleep in, without even a by-your-leave. No, missy, it's just not safe."

Jo didn't agree. They were so far off the beaten path that it wasn't likely anybody would leave the main road to find them. And while the Jones place was closer to town, she knew it was true about their lack of sleeping space for two more.

It seemed she was the only one who thought she and Andrew could stay at home. Mrs. Jones talked to the sheriff, Mr. Stanton, and he too thought they couldn't remain on the farm alone.

"Still some renegades running around loose," Mr. Stanton said. "No telling what they'll get into their heads. Your granny could handle that rifle, but you can't, missy. Why, right this minute we're out looking for a feller escaped from the prison right here in Huntsville. Dangerous man, he is, and no telling what he'd do if he happened on a pair of helpless young 'uns. No, staying out on that farm is out of the question. 'Twould be best if you went to stay with your uncle over to Muddy Wells until Miss Harriet can get here from Galveston."

That idea had been the most unwelcome idea yet, but Jo's protests were to no avail. Mr. Stanton had insisted. He had paid for the stage passage—"No doubt your uncle will reimburse me," he stated—and had even come out to get them to put them on it after he'd failed to find another family willing and able to take them in for the summer. Andrew was too young to be of any value as a laborer, which might have helped. And nobody, it seemed, had space for a twelve-year-old girl. Not when they already had a houseful of mostly boys; she couldn't share a room with *them*.

Jo remembered the last thing the sheriff had said, just before the coach pulled out. "It ain't likely the stage'll be robbed this trip, seeing as it was held up no more'n two weeks ago and the fellers that did it are now behind bars. You'll be better off with your uncle, you'll see."

Jo realized that the adult concerns were sincere, though she disagreed with their reasoning. Yet the matter had been taken entirely out of her hands.

The nearer they got to Muddy Wells, the more nervous Jo was getting about meeting their uncle, the judge. Especially since some of their fellow passengers had rather hinted that living with their uncle might not be all that they hoped for.

If only, Jo thought, she could get out her sketch pad and

draw to pass the time. She had tried, at first. She was quite good at faces and figures. Sometimes the people she drew didn't appreciate her efforts, though most did. There wasn't room, though, squashed together as they were, to hold the pad on her lap and have room for her right elbow to stick out in a drawing position. And the coach jostled them about so much that it was impossible to control her pencil. She had had to give up sketching except when they were stopped.

Mrs. Hilson had been flattered with the picture Jo had drawn of her, though Jo had been quite honest in her depiction of the overweight woman. She had drawn her smiling, so that she looked rather jolly, and when Jo offered her the finished version Mrs. Hilson folded it carefully and put it into her reticule.

"Never had a portrait of myself before," she said. "I shouldn't wonder but what it would make a nice present for Mr. Hilson."

For lack of anything else to do, while they waited for the horses to be changed and supper put out for the passengers, Jo drew Deputy Shaker. It was one of the best she'd ever done, she thought. There was his prominent Adam's apple, the high forehead, the wide mouth with a cigarette dangling from its corner.

Mrs. Hilson marveled over the likeness. "Imagine! A young 'un like you with so much talent! It's the spitting image of you, Deputy!"

Mr. Shaker rolled himself another smoke before he wandered over to where Jo sat on a rock with the sketch pad on her lap. She waited for his opinion, but he didn't give it voice. He simply grinned before he walked away to speak to the cook. She decided that meant that he liked it.

Sometimes Jo positively itched to draw. Once back on the

stage, it seemed as if drawing might make her forget how her bottom ached, and stop worrying about how things were going to be with the judge in Muddy Wells.

Andrew squirmed, and while Jo sympathized, she wished he could sit still. If he gave a quarter of an inch, Mrs. Hilson expanded into the space, and it was difficult to regain the lost territory.

Jo had never been more bored in her life.

And then, suddenly, everything changed.

A bullet plowed into the coach just above Jo's head. Up on top, the driver whooped, and cracked the whip over the backs of the horses, and the team bolted.

Mrs. Hilson screamed and doubled forward, almost carrying Jo off the seat with her. Jo had a glimpse of Mr. Levinger's face, turning white, and heard Deputy Shaker swear.

"Get down! Get your heads down!" he yelled, and even as Jo dove for the floor, dragging Andrew with her, she heard Mr. Doane cry out and knew he'd been hit in a second volley of shots.

Andrew's face was close to hers, down on a level with the men's boots. "We're being held up!" he cried, incredulous.

So much for Sheriff Stanton's conviction that they'd be safer going to Muddy Wells than staying on the farm. Jo's heart was trying to tear its way out of her chest, and she didn't have the breath to answer. She buried her face in her arms, heard Deputy Shaker's six-shooter go off over her head as he leaned out the window, and prayed for dear life that they wouldn't all be killed.

2

With Mrs. Hilson on the floor too there wasn't much room for anyone else. Jo couldn't count the number of shots that were fired; it was as if cannons were going off all around them, so that for a few moments she was deafened by the noise.

Andrew had his face straight down, on the undertaker's dusty boots, and his hands pressed over his ears. Beside Jo, Mrs. Hilson was gasping for breath but mercifully no longer emitting that earsplitting scream.

Deputy Shaker, who had been leaning out the window, withdrew to reload, but by the time he'd managed it, the horses were slowing.

Mr. Levinger moaned. "I've been shot! I'm bleeding!"

Cautiously, Jo turned her head, keeping it low. Sure enough, blood seeped between the man's fingers as he held his hand over one ear.

Nobody else was paying any attention to the injured man. The stagecoach jolted to a halt, and from outside a commanding voice shouted, "Everybody out! Come out with your hands up, and throw down your guns!"

Nobody moved, and then the door was jerked open. Mr.

Levinger, who had been leaning against it, virtually fell out, still clutching his dripping ear.

"The rest of you! Out!"

"I'm not armed! I'm injured," Mr. Levinger babbled, but the man holding a pair of enormous revolvers trained on them ignored him.

"Step down, make it smart, or I'll shoot the rest of you too!"

The firing had ceased. Jo lifted her head a bit higher and looked to the adults for guidance.

Deputy Shaker hesitated, then reluctantly tossed his six-shooter out the open doorway. "Better do as he says," he advised heavily.

"Don't shoot," Mr. Doane called. "We're coming out." He climbed over Jo and Andrew and stepped down, raising his hands over his head. "We have a lady aboard, sir. Allow me to assist her."

Jo sat up, drawing Andrew with her to avoid being trampled as Mrs. Hilson struggled to her feet. The woman was pale, but trying to maintain her composure as she allowed herself to be handed down.

"Now you two," Deputy Shaker said, and waited for Jo and Andrew to precede him.

Jo's legs were shaking when she finally stood on the bare ground and took stock of the situation. Her mouth was so dry she felt as if it were full of cotton. Dust swirled around them, for only seconds had passed and there were still horses in motion.

Five of them, Jo saw, and her artist's eye registered impressions even as she began to pray that they would only be robbed, not killed.

Five men, all on horses she would recognize if she saw

them again: one black stallion; two bays, a gelding and a mare; a powerful roan; and a sturdy, ugly paint with a walleye.

The bandits, of course, were masked. All that could be seen were their eyes and the narrow strips of deeply tanned skin between the bandannas tied over their lower faces and the brims of their hats.

Two sets of gray eyes, one set of brown, a pair that were almost without discernible color, and a pair that were a startlingly vivid blue.

Absorbing all of this took only moments. Mr. Levinger was still bemoaning his fate when the leader of the bandits suddenly turned his attention from the other passengers and spoke to him sharply. "Shut up! I'd as soon put a bullet between your eyes as to listen to you sniveling!"

Mr. Levinger gulped and fell silent in midsentence.

"My friend will pass among you," the leader said, "and relieve you of money, watches, and jewelry. I advise you to hold nothing back, because if I even suspect that that is the case, I will drop you where you stand. Everybody."

It took only seconds for that to sink in. One mistake could mean they would *all* be shot and left here to die.

The leader of the bandits gestured toward the stage driver with one of the guns. "Throw down the cashbox."

Jo had sketched Bill, the driver, too. He was a lean, dried-up man of about sixty, with a lined, brown face. Jo glanced at him now and saw that face contorted in pain. Bill was clutching his shoulder, and he too had blood between his fingers.

"Can't throw it down with a broke shoulder," he said angrily. "Git it yourself."

Another gesture was obviously an order to one of the marauders, who leaned out of the saddle to pull down the strongbox. It was heavy, and Jo wondered if it was full of gold. Not that she cared. She hoped the men would take it, and all the valuables belonging to the passengers, and leave them alone.

Deputy Shaker, just behind Andrew, spoke abruptly. "Let me tend to the driver before he bleeds to death."

"Leave your valuables in the bag," the man said, "and then relieve *him* of his, first."

The bandit who moved forward, holding open a leather pouch to receive their unwilling offerings, was the one with blue eyes. He was, Jo guessed, only a boy, for he was slight and sat more lightly in the saddle. Jo absorbed that without even being aware that she was noticing. She had suddenly remembered that she was wearing Mama's locket, and it was hanging in plain sight, right on the front of her blue-and-white checked gingham dress.

He couldn't take the locket, Jo thought in dismay. It contained the only likenesses of both Mama and Pa, and the locket itself was real gold.

Please, God, strike him dead, Jo begged silently, but the young man was holding out the bag toward Deputy Shaker, and God evidently did not find merit in Jo's plea.

Silently, his mouth a grim flat line, Mr. Shaker deposited his money pouch and his watch in the bag.

"Now his," the leader said, and Bill the driver handed over his own treasures, cursing.

Next in line was Mr. Doane, who could not resist a few words as he gave up his belongings. "You'll be sorry when you're caught," he suggested. "You'll come to trial before Judge Macklin, who knows just what to do with ruffians like you."

Jo sensed amusement on the face behind the mask; perhaps it was in the way the skin crinkled around the man's eyes.

"Ah, Macklin! The hanging judge! I've heard of him."

"You'll hear more," the undertaker predicted, letting go of his watch as if the action were painful.

The bandit shrugged. "Judges do not worry me. Now you, madam, and if you do not want my man to undress you to find it, pull out whatever's on the end of that gold chain and hand it over."

Mrs. Hilson's distress was clear. "Oh, please, take my purse, but not my only heirloom! It has great sentimental value—"

The man's voice cut through her near whimper. "And I am a sentimental man, madam."

In a sudden savage movement he kneed his mount toward her and leaned forward, reaching out for the part of the chain that was visible at the woman's neck. For a moment it appeared that he was going to shoot her, for the six-gun grazed her jaw, and then he snapped the chain.

Mrs. Hilson cried out involuntarily and put a hand to the raw place where the chain had cut into her flesh. There were tears in her eyes and her lips trembled as the bandit addressed her.

"You see, now it has sentimental value for *me* as well. Your purse, madam, or must I take that by force also?"

Jo felt cold. Could she remember their faces, Mama and Pa's, well enough to draw them from memory? Or would she have lost all that she had left of them, forever?

The young man with the pouch had reached Jo and Andrew. "Turn out your pockets," he told the little boy in a voice that was curiously soft, or perhaps he was attempting to disguise it.

Andrew obeyed with alacrity, for he had nothing to declare.

And then the blue eyes were fixed on Jo.

She felt strange, hot and cold at the same time, and her knees were wobbly, but she met his gaze squarely enough. She put up her hands to unfasten the chain, but hesitated, not dropping the locket into the outstretched pouch.

"Please," she said, and was ashamed that her voice squeaked, "take this, but let me keep the pictures. They aren't of any use to anyone but me, the portraits of my dead parents."

She thought she saw hesitation in the blue eyes, and quickly opened the golden oval with a thumbnail, but before she could begin to pry out the tiny sepia-tinted daguerreotypes, the leader lost patience.

"Enough of this nonsense! Drop it in the bag!" And before Jo could respond, he had once more nudged his horse forward, and slashed down with his gun barrel across the back of Jo's hand.

It was only a glancing blow; if it had landed solidly, it would surely have broken bones. As it was, the pain of it made her cry out and recoil from him.

She dropped the locket into the pouch and fought tears, swallowing hard to keep from letting him know how much it hurt.

Again her gaze met that of the young bandit, and for a moment she thought she detected a flicker of compassion.

Was there even a hint of apology as he urged in a soft tone, "Your money, miss?"

She had so little that it didn't matter when she handed it over, but she was sick at heart over the locket and its pictures.

She lowered her eyes, and through a blur of tears focused on the young bandit's hands. A scar, newly healing, ran across the back of the left one.

He was moving away now to the last passenger, Mr. Levinger. Though the injury to his ear might not be serious, it was obviously painful, and the poor man used to the civilities of Boston was having a difficult time dealing with the realities of frontier life in Texas.

He handed over money and watch without a sound. Jo thought he was as close to weeping as she was.

Andrew leaned against her and Jo put an arm around his shoulders and drew him closer. "Are they going to let us go?" Andrew wondered, and Jo could only wait to see what the bandits would do.

The blue-eyed one with the pouch had finished passing it among the passengers and pulled his mount around to face the leader. Jo followed him with her eyes, willing him to ride away with the others and leave them here to continue their journey into Muddy Wells.

"Give me the pouch," the leader said, and for an almost imperceptible moment the youngest bandit hesitated.

The leader's short temper flared again. "Give it here!" he exploded, and struck out once more with the barrel of one of his six-guns as he snatched the leather pouch.

The boy stifled a yip and let it go, but he was knocked to one side in such a way that his dusty hat nearly went off his head. And Jo saw his hair, which until then had been carefully concealed.

Red hair. *Flaming* red hair. The color hair she'd always wished she had, instead of an ordinary medium brown that she'd inherited from Mama.

Pa had had red hair. It had been a long time since Jo had seen it, but she remembered it as being almost like this, shining in the sun like a new copper penny. Jo wondered if anyone else had seen it.

The boy straightened in the saddle, clapped his hat back over the distinctive hair, and wheeled away.

The leader shouted, "Let's go!" and the others fell in behind him, galloping after the red-haired bandit, off across the prairie.

Jo watched them go, thanking God that they hadn't shot anyone again, feeling the ache in her hand where the gun barrel had grazed it. She wondered if the boy hurt too where the man had struck his shoulder.

Mr. Levinger was staring at Deputy Shaker. "Are you just going to let them get away with it? Robbing us, shooting us? Isn't that why you were traveling with us, to protect the stage and its passengers because there was another holdup recently?"

The deputy gave him a look of disdain. "What do you want me to do, take off after them by myself? With six shots for the five of them, all of us bouncing up and down so the chances of me hitting anybody range from slim to none? We got to get old Bill there to Doc Scobie and get that bullet out of his shoulder before he loses any more blood."

It appeared to Jo that he'd already lost a considerable amount, for Bill sat slumped in the high seat with his brown shirt now mostly a deep red.

"But they took every cent I had—over two hundred dollars!" Mr. Levinger protested. "Isn't a law officer supposed to try to get it back?"

"Soon's we get Bill to the doctor we'll round us up a posse," Mr. Shaker told him shortly. "Everybody back in the coach, let's go. You, missy," he said unexpectedly, looking at Jo, "you up to climbing up there beside Bill and holding something against that shoulder, in case he passes out?"

She was startled, but she wasn't afraid of the blood. She'd helped Grandma when she accidentally chopped her foot with an ax, and Andrew was always bleeding for one reason or another.

"Of course," she said, and allowed him to boost her up onto the high seat. "What about my petticoat?"

The deputy grunted assent, and when she raised her skirts he helped her tear a big chunk out of the undergarment. Before she'd even folded it into a pad to press against the place where the bullet had torn a hole through the shoulder, Mr. Shaker had grabbed the reins and vaulted up to sit on the other side of the stage driver.

He cracked the whip and the horses strained forward, almost before the passengers were settled inside.

There were shouts of protest when the deputy urged the team to a full gallop, but Mr. Shaker paid them no attention, and Jo saw the reason for his haste.

Bill had been managing to stay upright, but he was in such bad shape he'd have fallen had he not had Mr. Shaker on one side and Jo on the other to prop him up now. God had not answered her prayer to strike the bandits dead, but they hadn't done any more shooting. She decided to try another prayer on behalf of the stage driver.

She was busy trying to keep her seat and hold the pad in place to slow the bleeding; she didn't have time to pay much attention to the surroundings when they finally thundered into Muddy Wells. It was a great relief when they pulled up in front of the Grand Hotel, even though their own dust swirled around them in a choking cloud as soon as they stopped.

People came running along the street after them. Helpful hands lifted Bill down to carry him to the doctor's office, and then Deputy Shaker helped Jo down as well, leaving the rest of the passengers to their own devices.

Jo had just looked down at her front and realized what a mess she was, with Bill's blood on her dress and her torn petticoat dragging the ground, when she heard the deputy speak.

"Brought you a present, Judge. Two of 'em, actually."

She looked up, forgetting her clothes at the sight of an astonished face.

Judge Macklin looked very much like the picture of Grandpa Macklin that Grandma had treasured for as long as Jo could remember. Except that he had an astounded and unwelcoming expression that made Jo's blood chill a little.

"I'm Josephine," she said, and then the judge's face only grew more disbelieving. "Josephine Eleanor Elizabeth Whitman," she added. "Your mama was my grandma. My mama was your sister Stella."

To her total dismay this information did not erase the judge's expression of consternation at all. On the contrary, it seemed to make it worse.

"We've come to stay with you," Jo said uncertainly, wondering if Sheriff Stanton's letter had somehow gone astray. "Andrew and me. My little brother."

Deputy Shaker suddenly brayed with laughter. "I reckon you're a surprise to His Honor, missy."

Jo stared at the judge and her heart sank. A surprise, and an unwanted one at that.

Her throat closed and she couldn't think of anything else to say.

Welcome to Muddy Wells, she thought bleakly. It was going to be even worse than she'd expected.

3

Uncle Judge Matthew Macklin did not, after all, look quite like Grandpa, Jo decided. In the picture Grandpa had smiled for years and years. Jo had always thought of him as a kind and friendly man.

The judge did not look as if he had ever smiled.

He certainly was not smiling now.

"I was expecting two boys," he said, and his voice made Jo shiver. In just such a tone might he have sentenced a horse thief to be hanged.

Jo swallowed as she felt Andrew's hand creep into hers. "Well, my brother's a boy. I'm a girl."

"Obviously. Stella's children. Ma used to mention you. Andrew and Joe."

"I'm Jo. For Josephine Eleanor Elizabeth—"

Her uncle waved an impatient hand. "I heard you the first time. Why do you go by a boy's name, since you're clearly a female?" He seemed to suggest she had deliberately tried to deceive him.

Deputy Shaker had referred to "old Judge Macklin," but this man was not old. His hair was still dark brown, and he was slim and strong. If only he hadn't looked so stern he might have been considered handsome, but his mouth was flat and unyielding. Hostile, Jo decided, and wondered what she could do to soften that hostility.

"Jo is for Josephine," she repeated. "My name is too long, so everybody shortened it to Jo. Spelled with no *e* on the end of it."

He considered that as he would have considered the testimony in court of an accused cattle rustler. "I thought Ma just didn't spell very well," he said finally. And then, so glumly that Jo's heart sank even further, "A girl. What am I supposed to do with a *girl?*"

"We're only to stay until Aunt Harriet can come to—"

"That was a rhetorical question," he interrupted. "Sheriff Stanton shouldn't have put you on the stage before I had a chance to reply to his letter. I was hardly prepared to look after two boys, but a girl is impossible."

"Why?" Jo asked in confusion and humiliation, at the same time that Andrew said stoutly, "Jo can't help it she's a girl."

The judge ignored Andrew and answered Jo. "Because I'm a bachelor, to begin with. I don't know anything about raising girls."

"Well, I'm practically raised now," Jo pointed out. "And I'm used to looking after Andrew. . . ."

"I travel," the judge said, as if doggedly determined to bring forth every possible obstacle. "I'm a circuit-riding judge. I don't work only here in Muddy Wells, I go around a wide territory to hold court where I'm needed."

"We could go with you," Andrew said. "We're seasoned travelers now, after all that time on the stage."

Deputy Shaker was still standing there listening, looking amused. "Got you there, Judge. They stood up under a bone-jolting stage ride, dust thick enough to stand on, same beans and corn bread the rest of us et, and a stage robbery, to boot. Fact is, this young lady is quite plucky, sat right up there beside Bill and held a wad of her petticoat over the place where the bullet went into him, to keep him from bleeding to death before we got him here. Shouldn't wonder if she saved his life."

The judge gave him a sour look. "Coming from you, Shaker, that's quite a testimonial. What good was it having an armed deputy on board if you let the stage be held up?"

Deputy Shaker was not offended. "I had one six-shooter. There were five of them, each with a pair apiece. I wasn't on the stage to ride shotgun, Your Honor. I was on a business trip to the county seat."

Without thinking, Jo spoke up. "Only four of them were armed, sir. The one who collected our valuables in the pouch didn't have a gun."

"That right? Well, you're more observant than I was."

Mr. Levinger, having gotten his luggage down off the back of the stage, stepped forward and entered the conversation. "I hope you were observant enough to know those ruffians again when you catch up with them. If you're even going to *try*."

"Oh, I'm going to go after them," Mr. Shaker assured him, unruffled. "Soon as I see how Doc's coming with old Bill, I'll find the sheriff and we'll get us up a posse. When we bring them back, the judge here will see to it you get your money back if they haven't already spent it."

Mr. Levinger's mouth was pinched. "I can't tell you how grateful I am for your swift actions, Deputy. And how much confidence I have in you."

Sarcasm, Grandma would have called that, but Jo thought the deputy had done what he could. He wouldn't have had a chance against all those other guns. It wouldn't have helped anybody if the bandits had shot and killed Mr. Shaker.

Mr. Levinger glanced across the street. "If someone will direct me to this doctor, perhaps he can do something about my ear after he's attended to the driver. If," he concluded bitterly, "such a trifling wound is considered worthy of attention in this barbaric place."

"Doc's office is the little one in the middle," Judge Macklin informed him. "Between the saloon and the bank. I expect he'll treat even a Yankee, though your injury does appear trifling." He ignored Mr. Levinger's spluttering. "How much did you see of these bandits, Shaker? You think they were the same gang that wiped out the bank two weeks ago?"

Clearly peeved that no one thought his injured ear was important, Mr. Levinger turned and walked across the street, dodging some of the sightseers who were gathered around the coach to listen to Mrs. Hilson and Mr. Doane recite the details of their ordeal.

Deputy Shaker pulled out his tobacco pouch and began to roll a smoke while he considered this. He would never have been allowed in Grandma's house; she despised tobacco and couldn't abide the smell of it. But Jo had decided she liked the deputy. It was too bad *he* wasn't the one who was their uncle instead of this rigid, unwelcoming man.

"Somebody hit the stage over near Huntsville couple of weeks ago. Might be the same gang, and if they'll rob stages, they might rob banks as well. Reckon I'd know the horses again," the deputy said finally. "Wasn't much to be seen of the bandits. Same kind of clothes everybody wears, nothing special about them. Hats covering their heads, bandannas over their faces. Young one's hat got knocked askew, he had red hair. You see any more than that, missy?"

Jo was pleased that he thought enough of her opinion to ask. "Not much," she had to confess. "The horses would be easier to identify. But the leader had a ring on his left hand, a big silver one with carving on it. A bronco, I think. I mean, the head of one carved on it." She hadn't even realized she'd noted that at the time, but when she thought about drawing the man, she remembered the ring. "He was big too. Bigger than either one of you."

The judge made a snorting sound. "Well, you bring 'em in and we'll see they don't rob any more stages. Got the cashbox clean away, I suppose."

"Sure did," Deputy Shaker admitted. "I'm surprised old Mr. Murphy ain't already boiling out of the bank wanting to know where his money is. Bill let on it was a pretty good haul."

"I hope he didn't let on where some of those rogues overheard him," the judge observed. "Murphy would scalp him if he thought a stage driver was giving away secrets that got his cashbox lifted. You better get on with recovering it."

"Right. Whole town must know the stage was robbed by this time. I'll get me some grub, and by that time ought to be a posse put together."

He looked at Jo and touched two fingers to the brim of his hat, just as if she were a grown-up lady. "It was nice traveling with you, missy. Too bad those bandits covered up their faces, or you could draw us up some wanted posters and we'd have the whole county knowing who to look for. You take care of the judge, now. He could use a female touch around his place." He grinned and walked away, but the judge still wasn't smiling.

"What did he mean by that?"

Jo put her hand up to touch the locket, the way she sometimes did when she was nervous, but of course it was no longer there. "I don't know. Sir. Does your house need to be cleaned?"

Her uncle gave her a look that said clearly he was still hostile. "I didn't mean *that*. He's a bachelor too. What does he know about housekeeping? Besides, I have Mrs. Bacon come in for that. I meant about you drawing wanted posters?"

"Jo draws real good," Andrew piped up. "Show him the picture of Deputy Shaker, Jo."

Silently, she took the folded paper out of her reticule—the one that had once belonged to Grandma—and handed it over.

The judge opened it up and studied it. Something in his face shifted, changed, perceptibly. Jo thought perhaps it was respect she saw in his eyes when he glanced back at her. "I'd recognize him anywhere," he conceded. And then, as if he'd been too free with his approval, he added, "His Adam's apple's a bit bigger than that."

Jo didn't answer. Nobody else who'd seen the picture had said any such thing, and she was tired of standing around in a bloody dress, and hungry besides.

"Are we going to stay here on the street the whole rest of the day, Uncle Matthew? Our trunk is still up on the back of the stage." Now that the crisis was over, she was beginning to shake. She wanted to go home, wherever that was.

His look said he didn't like her very much, but Jo told herself she didn't care. She'd only be here a short time, and she could stand him that long, same as he could stand her. Kin were supposed to stick together, Mama always said, and she'd tried to get Grandma to make up with Aunt Harriet. Jo had always believed Grandma was pretty stubborn, to stay mad at a daughter for years because she married a man Grandma didn't like. It was easy to see where Uncle Matthew got his stubbornness, so she supposed she had to make allowances.

Any civil kin would take in his sister's orphaned children after his ma died and couldn't take care of them anymore. So when the judge didn't move, she turned and pointed out the trunk. "That one. With the brass bands on it."

To her relief the judge got it down. "I recognized it," he said, settling it on his shoulder. "Ma had it from the time I was younger than this one."

"My name's Andrew," the little boy reminded him, but the judge still didn't say his name, just grunted. "My wagon's over there. Come along."

It was a nice wagon, though excessively dusty, like everything else in Muddy Wells. Jo thought cleaning the seat was too big a job to do with a handkerchief, and since she was already a mess, she could hardly damage her skirts any further by sitting on a dusty wagon seat. While the judge loaded the trunk in the wagon bed along with bags of feed and flour and a saddle, she climbed up and sat down.

Andrew hesitated, looking up from the board sidewalk. "Aren't we going to find out how the stage driver is?"

"Of course. Run across the street, there where the people are standing around, and ask," Jo told him.

The judge didn't countermand the order, but he couldn't resist a comment as he climbed up beside Jo and picked up the reins. "If there's one thing I can't stand, it's a bossy female."

Stung, Jo retorted, "And you don't think there's any other kind."

It was a challenge, flung right in his face as good as Grandma would have done it, and Jo hadn't backed down any more than Grandma would have. Funny, she hadn't thought of herself as being anything like Grandma at all; but since the old lady was gone, she'd found herself being quite a lot like her.

The judge gave her a level look. "Your ma was always my favorite of the family. Nice, pleasant girl, she was. She wasn't bossy, and she didn't talk back."

"I'm not my mama," Jo informed him. "I'm me. Josephine Eleanor Elizabeth Whitman. I'm not even a Macklin."

He made a snorting sound. "Oh, yes, you are. Spitting image of Ma, no matter what your pa's name was. Ma and my sister Harriet still feuding, were they, right to the end?"

"I guess so. Grandma wouldn't even write to her when she knew she was dying. It was the neighbors insisted I do that. You needn't worry, you won't be stuck with us for long. Only until Aunt Harriet can take us."

"You know Harriet?" His glance was quizzical.

It was the most civil thing he'd said to her so far.

"Not really. Only from her letters to Mama."

"You think Ma was bossy—that where you got that way?—wait'll you see Harriet. She like to drove me crazy with her orders when I was a boy. 'Wash your hands, scrape the mud off your boots, clean your plate, fetch the eggs, go to bed, get up.' Never gave me a minute's peace."

"I reckon you needed to be told what to do, just like Andrew," Jo said coolly, though her heart was pounding and she wished he'd turned out to be kind and jolly, the way Papa had been.

To her total surprise, Uncle Judge Matthew laughed. Out loud.

It made his face quite different. Jo didn't know how to react to it. He was still chuckling when Andrew came running back across the street, and he reached down a hand to help him swing into the back of the wagon.

"How's Bill doing?"

"The doctor has the bullet out," Andrew reported, settling between two feed bags. "He says Bill's going to be all right. He just lost a lot of blood, but his shoulder's not broke after all. He can't drive stage for a few days, though."

The judge looked at Jo as he slapped the reins over the

rumps of the team and they began to roll. "You draw any more of those pictures?"

"She did Mrs. Hilson," Andrew offered. "But she liked it so well she kept it, for her husband."

"Hmm," the judge said. "Like the deputy said, it's a pity those men had their faces covered so you didn't see them. Ah, well. The posse will catch up with them, no doubt, and when they do we'll put an end to their greedy ways."

"Will you hang them?" Andrew asked eagerly.

"I'm only the judge. Jury has to decide they're guilty, first. Whoa!" he interrupted himself, pulling on the reins.

"Good afternoon, Judge," said the lady he'd just barely avoided running over.

The judge tipped his hat. "Afternoon, Miss Brown. You want to be more careful, stepping out into the street that way."

Jo couldn't tell from his tone whether he was annoyed or not. She studied the lady, who was rather youngish but not a *girl* anymore. She was pretty, and had brown hair that was drawn up into a cluster of ringlets atop her head. The lady's eyes were friendly as they rested first upon Jo, then Andrew, then moved back to the judge.

"But I wanted you to stop, so I could meet these young people."

To meet us so she could have an excuse to talk to *him*, Jo thought immediately.

"My sister's young 'uns," the judge said. "Josephine Eleanor Elizabeth Whitman, and her brother, Andrew."

Miss Brown was smiling, the kind of smile that made you want to smile back. "Hello. I'm Susan Brown, and I teach school here in Muddy Wells. I hope to see both of you when school starts again."

"They won't be here," the judge said brusquely. "My sister Harriet will take them before then."

"Oh. Well, in church, then. You *will* be bringing them to church, won't you?"

"We always went to church at home," Jo said quickly. "Grandma said it would be wicked to raise children and not see to their spiritual needs by taking them to services on Sundays."

"Naturally," the judge said, and though she could tell he was being sarcastic again, she wasn't sure he was actually angry about it. "All right, I'll see that they're in church Sunday morning."

"Good! I'll see you all then," Miss Brown said brightly, and went across the street before they drove on.

There wasn't much conversation the rest of the way, except when one of them asked a question. They learned that Judge Macklin owned and ran the Muddy Wells Mercantile, on the main street, and lived on a small ranch on the edge of town, which was a surprise to both the children. They had thought he was only a judge, nothing more.

"Can't make a living just being a judge in the state of Texas," he said dryly. "The yearly salary wouldn't give a man enough to gladden the preacher's heart if you dropped the whole thing into his collection plate at once. That's home up there, in the middle of that stand of cottonwoods."

Although she'd been terribly disappointed so far in Muddy Wells—one street three blocks long, lined with weary-looking buildings with the paint scoured off by the wind and the sand—if they'd ever been painted in the first place—Jo couldn't help leaning eagerly forward to see where they would be living.

Not in cool, shady piney woods, the kind that made her homesick every time she thought about them. But the cottonwoods *did* make shade around the house, so it would be a little cooler in the heat of the day.

There were no flowers, only a bare dirt yard with some chickens scratching around that ran squawking as the wagon rolled into their midst.

The house, however, was painted white and had a veranda across the front of it. A pair of hounds rose lazily from the steps, wagging their tails, and came to meet them.

"It's bigger than Grandma's house," Andrew observed, jumping down and automatically scratching behind the ears of each of the dogs. "Aunt Harriet ought to come here to live, where there's more room."

The judge gave him a startled glance. "Not on your life! Here, you take these little packages, boy, and you, girl, open up the front door for him. I'll go on out to the barn and unload the rest of this feed."

Jo had the feeling that if she didn't assert herself this new relative would very quickly reduce them to ciphers. "Our names," Jo said clearly, "are Andrew and Josephine—"

"All right, all right, don't go through that whole list again! Go on inside, I'll be back to carry in the trunk!"

The dogs followed them into the parlor, which looked as if nobody ever sat in it. There were no pictures as on Grandma's walls, nor antimacassars on the backs of the chairs and sofas, nor potted plants. In fact, it looked as if it had never been lived in.

They kept going, however, following the hounds into the kitchen. Here, it was clear, was where the living was done.

A scrawny little woman, about the size Grandma had been and only a few years younger, turned to greet them.

"Well, my stars, here you are! And one of you's a girl!"

This lady didn't make it sound as if being a female was a curse. She was wearing an apron over her flower-print dress, and her face looked as if it smiled a lot. The kitchen was filled with the aroma of baking corn bread and simmering beans and ham. "I'm Mrs. Bacon. I come in once a week to do for the judge, poor man. I knew you were supposed to arrive today, so I thought I'd leave you a bite to eat. The judge just about lives on nothing, poor soul. Can't be bothered to cook. Can you cook, dear?"

Jo felt at home with her at once. "Yes, ma'am. Grandma taught me how to cook."

"Good! Good! Here, young fellow, give me those bundles and I'll see where they go. Sugar, coffee, molasses, yes."

She bustled about, putting things away, showing Jo where everything was kept. Jo couldn't resist a question, because the judge hadn't seemed to her a poor soul at all.

"Why do you feel sorry for Uncle Matthew?" she asked.

"Oh, dear, you haven't heard the story, I suppose. Not much for writing to his ma, was he? And now she's gone, more's the pity. Be nice if people showed their feelings while everybody's still alive, but after they're buried and it's too late, many of them wish they had a second chance to make up, don't they? Felt really bad, the judge did, when he heard his ma had died."

Jo agreed it would have been nice if he'd told Grandma he cared about her, for now it was, indeed, too late. Though Grandma was in heaven, of course, and maybe people in heaven knew what was happening down below. At least she hoped they did. Sometimes she still talked to Mama and Grandma, as if they could hear her.

"No, ma'am, what's the story?" she asked, and Mrs. Bacon nodded.

"It's only right you should know it, and *he'll* never tell you. Disappointed in love, he was."

"The judge?" Jo asked, disbelieving.

"Oh, yes. Happened four years ago, and would you believe, he's never looked at another woman since? Was all set to marry the lady when she jilted him, practically at the altar. Ran off with a traveling man, she did. He's never gotten over it. He was fixing up this house for her, and then she never came to live in it. Different sort of man he was, then. Not so dour as he is now. But inside, he's a nice man. Kind, you know."

Kind. Well, I'll have to be convinced of that, Jo thought; but she could understand how a broken heart could cause a man to sour. Somewhat, perhaps, the way Mama had drooped after Pa was killed. Of course Mama had had Jo and Andrew, so she hadn't gone sour like the judge, only sad. Jo decided to give her uncle a second chance, in case her first impression was in error.

By the time the judge showed up, and the hounds ran to leap up around him, Jo felt comfortable with Mrs. Bacon and less apprehensive about her uncle. She knew what it was like to hurt; if that was the judge's problem, she would follow Grandma's formula for healing the pain.

They all sat down to eat supper together. The judge had already reached for a slab of Mrs. Bacon's golden brown corn bread when Jo said firmly, "Bow your head, Andrew, while we say grace."

Out of the corner of her eye, she saw Uncle Matthew hesitate, then put down his knife and bow his head.

Jo smiled a little, inside herself, as she asked the blessing.

4

Andrew sat on the edge of the bed that Mrs. Bacon had made up for him in an upstairs room. He watched moodily, picking at the yarn ties on the colorful quilt, as Jo put his small store of clothes into the heavy old dresser drawers.

"I don't want to stay here," Andrew said. "I don't like Uncle Matthew."

Jo closed the drawer and turned toward him, pausing to look out the window toward the corral. "He has some nice horses, Andrew. Maybe he'll let us ride them."

"He didn't want us to come even when he thought we were both boys. He doesn't like us being here. Why doesn't he like us?"

Jo was watching the horses, knowing she'd have to sketch them. "It isn't personal, I guess. I mean, he's unhappy in love, didn't you hear what Mrs. Bacon said? And that makes him unhappy about everything."

"But it's not our fault, so why should he take it out on us?" Andrew scowled at the unfairness of it.

"That's the way grown-ups do sometimes. Remember how snappy Grandma used to be sometimes when her bones got to aching bad? We'll have to give Uncle Matthew a chance to get to know us, and then maybe he'll like us."

She didn't know if that would ever happen or not, but she wanted to make her brother feel better. "Besides, we won't be here for long."

Andrew flopped back on the bed, spread-eagled. "What if we don't like Aunt Harriet, either? *He* doesn't like her, and Grandma said she was a fool."

That didn't really bother Jo. "That was because she married a man Grandma said was shiftless and lazy. It wasn't because Aunt Harriet wasn't nice. Mama loved her. Remember how she laughed and cried over her letters?"

"I'll never understand grown-ups," Andrew decided. "What are we supposed to do now?"

Jo closed the lid on the trunk and headed for the doorway. "I'm going downstairs and ask Mrs. Bacon about that. Maybe we could go meet the horses."

She paused to glance into the room where she'd already put away her own belongings. She'd never had a room all to herself before, but the lump in her throat wouldn't go away. She wondered if she'd ever stop feeling homesick, and she was glad Aunt Harriet had decided to move to Huntsville. At least by the end of the summer she would be back there in familiar surroundings; but since Grandma and Mama were both gone now, it would never be the same.

She wondered if the judge was right about Aunt Harriet, that she was really as bossy as he remembered her.

Well, Jo thought, she was nearly grown now. No doubt one of these days soon she'd meet a young man who'd ask her to marry him—Mama had been no more than fifteen when she married Pa—and she'd have a cabin of her own somewhere. She wouldn't have to live with Aunt Harriet after that.

Jo had imagined that cabin of her own many times. Like most young couples, she and her new husband would probably start with one room. It would be small and snug, with a good fireplace for cooking and heat. There would be a scrubbed pine table with at least two chairs, and a bed with the quilt on it that Mama had made for her, the same one she'd carried in the trunk and put on the bed here so that it would feel more like home.

It didn't, though, Jo thought as she went on down the stairs. It felt very strange and different. It would have been much nicer if Uncle Matthew had been welcoming.

Mrs. Bacon had finished her chores. She would be back next week, as usual, she told Jo, but if they needed her help before then, or her advice, she could be found in her own house only a short walk to the east.

Jo's thanks were sincere, but she didn't think she would need help or advice.

The judge was sitting at the kitchen table with a ledger and a stack of papers spread out before him. He was scowling, but if he did that most of the time she couldn't wait for him to be in a better mood before she dared to speak to him. She cleared her throat. He didn't look up, but she addressed him, anyway.

"Is it all right if we go out and look at the horses?"

That brought his head up with a snap. "Don't you kids go fooling around the horses. You'll get your necks broken."

Jo paused beside the table, unable to keep the scorn out of her voice even though she knew she must show respect. "We can both ride."

He snorted. "Those old plow horses Ma used to keep?

These aren't that kind of horses. I'd have to go with you the first time, at least, and right now I'm too busy. I've got a court case tomorrow, and I need to have the books caught up to leave with old Maples."

Disappointed, Andrew made a hopeful suggestion. "You could take me to see the horses and Jo could add up the figures. She's real good with sums."

The judge gave Jo a speculative look, as if evaluating her intelligence. "How good?" he asked.

"Very good," Jo said. "I'm good at sums and reading and writing too."

He shoved a sheet of paper at her, dipped his pen in the inkwell, and thrust it at her. "Write something," he commanded.

Provoked, Jo wondered how come Grandma hadn't made him learn to say please and thank you, as she'd taught everyone else. Without comment, she took the pen and wrote, "Vengeance is mine; I will repay, saith the Lord."

She hadn't expected him to take the message personally, as she secretly meant it, but from the expression on his face she suspected that maybe he did. He took the pen back, wrote down a list of numbers, and handed the pen back.

"Add those," he directed.

Jo took the pen again, and added the column of figures quickly and accurately. She compressed her lips while he checked her addition.

The judge made an odd little sound, then pursed his lips. "You *like* adding up numbers?" he asked.

"Not for all day. But yes, for a period of time, I enjoy it." Jo hesitated, then added, "Grandma always said a person likes to do what he does well."

The judge suddenly grinned. "And so you might as well

learn to like to work, because you're going to have to earn a living, and you might as well begin right now. I was seven years old when she told me that."

"I was six," Jo stated.

"Good old Ma," the judge said. "She drove me crazy when I lived at home, never let me sit down for a minute to rest. But I kind of miss her. Miss knowing that she's still there, back home."

"You could have written to her once in a while," Jo pointed out.

He sighed, his amusement gone. "I never was one for writing much." He scrawled something on the paper, beside Jo's biblical quotation, and turned it so she could read it.

Only she couldn't. She screwed up her face and squinted. Andrew stepped forward and squinted too.

"Is that all the better you can write?" he asked, astonished.

"That's it," the judge agreed. "It's mortifying to write a letter to your ma and have her write back that she couldn't make out what you said. Mr. Hallows, the schoolmaster, used to smack my knuckles with a ruler when he couldn't read my spelling tests. I suppose Mr. Hallows died a long time ago."

"Yes. Mama said he smacked her with a ruler once too."

"He smacked me a lot more than once." The judge rubbed his knuckles as if they still stung. "I was trying my best to write so he could read it. I never did figure out how he thought hitting me would make me able to write better."

Jo picked up the paper and held it at eye level, squinting at it now from the new angle. "For God so loved the world, He gave his only begotten son, so that whosoever believeth in Him should not perish, but have everlasting life," she read aloud. "John 3:16!" So he *did* remember part of what Grandma had taught him.

He took the paper from her and examined it the same way Jo had. "Ma teach you to read it that way?"

"No. I figured it out for myself. Accidentally," Jo felt compelled to confess.

"Hmm. Well"—he turned to Andrew—"you want to see the horses, eh?"

"Yes, please," Andrew said eagerly.

The judge looked at Jo. "You willing to add up the rest of these figures?"

"Yes," Jo assented. She wanted to see the horses too, but she figured Andrew wanted it worse, and besides, if she didn't do the adding, neither of them would be allowed to go to the corral.

So she sat there in the kitchen working with the ledger until the judge and Andrew came back. The little boy's eyes were shining. "I got to ride Jury," he announced enthusiastically. "Uncle Matthew said I can ride him again tomorrow, when he comes home from the trial."

So much for hating Uncle Matthew, Jo thought wryly. Well, she didn't *hate* him. She didn't actually *like* him yet, but perhaps that would come when they got better acquainted. If the woman he had expected to marry and bring to this house as his bride had run off with a traveling man, she supposed it might have given him a jaundiced view of females in general. She would simply have to see what she could do to change his mind.

When the judge announced that it was time to turn in, Andrew started up the stairs, then paused to look back. "Aren't you going to come up and hear my prayers?" he asked.

The judge looked startled. "I don't know anything about that. Your sister can do it."

"Josephine," Jo encouraged him, more gently than Grandma would have done.

"Josephine," he echoed. "Let her do it. You can't expect me to get the hang of this being an uncle all at once. Besides, I always had the impression it was God you wanted to listen to your prayers, not some disinterested stranger."

They all jumped when there was a sudden banging on the front door.

"Now who in tarnation is that, at nine o'clock at night?" the judge asked, striding to open the door. Assuming that was another rhetorical question he didn't expect her to answer, Jo remained silent, but she waited at the foot of the stairs.

The young woman who stood there was carrying a baby in her arms, and her face looked worried.

"I'm sorry to come tell you this, Judge, but Ezra ain't going to be able to take over at the Mercantile tomorrow. He done broke his leg."

Jo guessed this to be Mrs. Old Maples, and since she was clearly no more than twenty, she guessed as well that old Maples was not old, either. It must simply be the way people talked in this part of Texas.

Jo watched as her uncle slowly turned a deep red. "Broke his leg? What in heaven's name did he want to go and do that for?"

"He didn't go to do it a'purpose, Judge," the young woman said earnestly, patting the baby as it began to whimper. "He fell off the shed roof. I reckon he's going to be laid up for quite a spell." Then, as if afraid to hear his reaction to that, she added hurriedly, "I got to get back home to see to him, sir," bobbed her head, and was gone.

Jo had heard men swear before, but never any more thoroughly than Uncle Matthew did it.

He stood staring at the empty doorway, asking another of the seemingly endless rhetorical questions. "And so now what am I supposed to do? Have the trial in the store and measure out sugar and flour while I listen to the witnesses?"

Jo saw the perfect opportunity to sway his opinion of females, and spoke boldly. "I'll tend the Mercantile. I know all about working in a store. I helped Mr. Sansome back home."

On the bottom step, Andrew opened his mouth, perhaps to remind her that she had only done it once, when Mr. Sansome had severely burned his hand and was having trouble doing everything with his left hand.

Before he could reveal the limited extent of her experience, Jo surreptitiously reached out and pinched him. Andrew gave her an aggrieved look but closed his mouth.

The judge was weighing her offer. "You're pretty young to be in complete charge."

"But all I have to do," Jo said, "is help them pick out the merchandise they want, take their money, give them change if they have it coming—or write it up on their bill—and write the sale in the ledger. And then total up the columns," she added, having gotten the message that he was not only slower than she was at adding but he disliked doing it.

It didn't take him long to make up his mind. "All right," he said, "but just for tomorrow. If Maples is going to be laid up for months, I'll have to find someone else as soon as possible, but I can't do that before tomorrow morning. Be up in time to leave the house by seven-thirty," he said, and turned away.

Not a please, not a thank-you, not even a good-night, Jo noted. It was a good thing Grandma wasn't around to see how poor her son's manners were. But she felt a little better.

She still had to prove herself, she knew that, but she was confident she could handle a general store for a day. Then perhaps her uncle would concede that females were good for something.

She heard Andrew's prayers, which consisted mostly of a plea that he would be able to ride the horse called Jury—what a name for a horse!—every day while they were in Muddy Wells. After that, Jo got undressed and crawled into the unfamiliar bed. It was too hot to pull the quilt over her, even though she had opened the window, and for a long time she lay unable to sleep, wishing Grandma hadn't died, wishing they hadn't had to come here where they weren't welcomed, wishing they were back in the Piney Woods.

She didn't even say any prayers of her own. Nothing she wanted was even possible now, at least for the moment, and she'd already thanked Him that none of them had been killed when the stage was held up. She didn't feel like thanking Him for having been taken in by the judge. She wasn't at all certain that it was going to be a blessing.

The last thing she remembered thinking about was the young bandit who had held the bag for her to drop her valuables into.

She would recognize that red hair, she thought, if she ever saw it again.

She couldn't have guessed just how soon that would be.

5

Jo was downstairs early and had breakfast on the table when Uncle Matthew and Andrew appeared. The larder was well supplied, and she'd had no trouble finding things to cook: ham and eggs and a stack of light, fluffy flapjacks, and plenty of good strong coffee.

The judge wore a black suit with a string tie. His boots could have stood a coat of polish, but she decided to ignore that this morning. She didn't want to rock the boat at a time when he might decide to leave her home.

"Good morning," Jo said, when he didn't greet her first.

"Morning. You didn't find the maple syrup. It's in a jug, in the bucket down the well with the butter. Only way to keep the ants out of it," he said, and sat down as if he had fully expected all along to be cooked for and waited on.

Andrew was dispatched to the well for syrup and the butter, and Jo carried the platters to the table and sat down. She bowed her head and said grace, the short one Grandma had used when the food was getting cold because of some delay. Uncle Matthew had already speared a piece of ham, but he had the courtesy to pause until Jo opened her eyes.

"Real fresh butter," he said, cutting a slab of it to put on top of the stack of flapjacks. "Don't often see butter in Texas. Everybody says it's too much work to make it right. But we have German neighbors, and they know how to do it. They bring me a pound or so a week." He observed the amount that both Andrew and Jo had added to their pancakes. "Maybe I better ask them to double my order."

Jo hoped they would, because it was delicious. She knew how hard it was to make it too, because she'd often been the one to use the churn until Andrew got big enough to do it. The judge didn't comment on the cooking, but he ate two stacks of the flapjacks and drank three cups of coffee besides devouring the ham and eggs.

"Andrew's going with me to the Mercantile," Jo announced when they had finished. "He can help put up stock or something, if you have anything that isn't already on the shelves."

"There's always something that isn't yet on the shelves," the judge assured her. "Got a shipment on the stage yesterday, two crates in the back room."

"Are the prices marked so I'll know how much to charge?"

"Some of them. For the rest, you can look back in the ledger and see what I charged before."

Jo cleared the table and put the dishes in the basin to do later. Grandma wouldn't have approved leaving them, but the judge didn't seem to notice. She hoped she'd be able to read what was written in the ledger.

"Does Mr. Maples work for you all the time?" she asked, making sure Andrew's mouth was wiped before he got down from the table.

"No, most of the time he's a farmer. He works on the days I'm holding court or have to go out of town. He's paying off his bill for the seed he planted this spring. He's not the brightest fellow around, but he was the best I could do at the time, and it seemed like a good way to collect what he owes me. Is everybody ready to go?"

Back home they would have walked such a short distance—Grandma didn't believe in wearing out the horses when they had perfectly good strong legs of their own—but the judge drove the buggy.

"Is there a courthouse where you'll hold the trial?" Jo wanted to know as they drove along Main Street.

"No. Not yet. But we don't have that many trials in Muddy Wells. So we hold court in the Silver Dollar."

"The saloon?" Jo questioned. Somehow that didn't seem appropriate for a court of law.

"The only other place in town that's big enough would be the church," the judge informed her. "And the preacher is always over there practicing his sermons, or the ladies' aid society is there for a meeting, or the organist is trying out next Sunday's hymns. So it's easier in the saloon. Not too many men drinking there at nine in the morning, and if there are, we can round up a jury before they've had too much to be of any use."

Once more Jo withheld her opinion of the system. She wouldn't want to rely on a bunch of drunks to decide whether a person went to prison, was hanged, or set free.

"What kind of case is it?" Andrew asked as they stopped in front of the Mercantile. "A murder?"

"Just as bad. Horse thieves."

That didn't require an explanation. Everybody knew that stealing a man's horse, in the right circumstances, could be condemning that man to death by thirst or starvation or rattlesnake bite. The penalty was the same as if the culprit had shot his victim in the back.

"You two get down here. I'll take the horses over to the

livery stable and meet you back here in a few minutes. I'll show you what to do in the store before it's time for the trial to begin."

Andrew piped up from his seat between the other two. "How come you use the livery stable when you're so close to home?"

The judge's tone was sardonic. "Only way to get any value for the money old Bergdahl owes me for *his* grocery and feed bill. Here, take the key and let yourselves in. I'll be there in a minute."

Jo and Andrew unlocked the door of the Muddy Wells Mercantile and stood inside, looking around at the boxes and barrels, crates and cans of merchandise.

"I smell licorice," Andrew said hopefully.

"We don't have any money to buy any." Jo's tone was thoughtful. "I wonder if the judge has to take all his profits in services, instead of cash."

"There's boots, Jo. Look, aren't these about my size?"

"We haven't any money," she repeated patiently. She knew how he felt. She saw things she would have liked too. For instance, some of that bolt of calico with the roses on it for a new dress, or one of those straw bonnets with the pink ribbons.

They had closed the door behind them and now turned as it opened to let in Deputy Shaker. He touched his fingertips to the brim on his hat when he saw Jo.

"Morning. I thought maybe the judge would be here. I need to know when he wants the prisoner brought over to the courtroom."

"In the saloon."

"Right. I choose not to produce the prisoners until the judge is about ready to proceed with the jury selection. Sometimes, if I think the feller's a wild one, I don't bring him over from the jail until we got the jury all picked. Too many ways out of there, and there's only the sheriff and me to guard two doors and four different windows."

Andrew was staring at him. "I thought you'd be out with a posse after the men who held up the stage."

The deputy reached over and picked two cigars out of a box on the long counter, then dug in his pocket for a nickel and put it down in payment. "Oh, we got up a posse, all right. Eight men, including me. We rode out and picked up the trail easy enough. But the men we was chasing took to the rocks there by the river and we lost 'em. Couldn't decide whether they went upstream or down, and it was getting too dark to see where they came out of the water, so we turned around and rode home."

"And that's all you did? You gave up and let them go?" Andrew was clearly disillusioned.

"Couldn't have tracked 'em on rocks, in the water, and at night, boy. Going home was only sensible."

"But won't they rob another stage?"

"More than likely," the deputy agreed. "Or rob a bank, maybe. When they do, we'll get 'em."

Jo wasn't sure she saw the logic of that last part; if they didn't catch them for one crime, why would they be able to catch them for another? But apparently the posses were successful at least part of the time.

"Did you catch the man they're trying today?" she asked politely.

"That I did," he said with satisfaction, putting the cigars into his shirt pocket. "One of 'em, anyway. Not the horse thief. Judge decided to try both men today and get it over with. We can use the same jury."

"What did he do?" Andrew wanted to know, intrigued by this real-life lawman even if he was disappointed about the failure of the posse last night.

"Shot and killed a man in a fight. Got fourteen witnesses, so it shouldn't take long to convict him, but he's entitled to trial by a jury of his peers." He considered his own statement for a moment before adding, "Come to think of it, for a jury to be of Weasel Willy's peers, we'd have to round up all the drunks, horse thieves, and polecats in the county. Willy's been making himself obnoxious for the last couple of years. We're pretty sure he's shot people before, but this is the first time we've had witnesses. Oh, here's the judge himself—you ready for the first prisoner, Your Honor?"

Judge Macklin nodded. "Give me ten minutes to get out the cashbox and tell Josephine a few things. Did he sleep off his drunk?"

"Yes, he's sober. Got a terrible headache, I reckon, but he's sober. Doesn't help his personality much, though."

He had said this quite cheerfully. The judge wasn't especially cheerful, however, as he made some quick explanations to Jo about a few things.

He didn't really think she could do a good job of running the store alone, she realized. He expected he'd come back to a pure mess. Well, she thought determinedly, he wouldn't.

For the first quarter of an hour after he'd gone, no one came in at all. Then an old lady showed up and bought a spool of thread, and a younger one bought a pound of sugar and two eggs. She was, she told Jo, going to make her little boy a cake for his third birthday.

Jo remembered her last birthday, when Grandma had made *her* a cake and even put two candles on it, because they didn't have a dozen. She wasn't a child any longer, and it shouldn't have bothered her that probably she'd never have another birthday cake unless she made it herself, but it did. Making your own cake wouldn't be any fun. She supposed, as she dutifully entered the last sale in the ledger, that when you were grown up you couldn't expect things to be fun anymore.

"Jo! Come here, quick!"

The urgency in Andrew's voice brought her to peer out the window at a pair of riders ambling along Main Street. One was a big man on a black stallion, the other little more than a boy, riding a horse she surely had seen before: a sturdy but ugly paint. If she could view it from the front, Jo knew it would be walleyed.

"It's them, isn't it?" Andrew demanded in an excited whisper. "The men who robbed the stage?"

Jo felt a sick shakiness sweep over her. She wet her lips. "I can't leave the store untended. Go out the back door, and around the end of the building. Tell the judge, or Deputy Shaker, or the sheriff—they're all in the saloon! And Andrew, don't let those men see you!"

Andrew gave a scared bob of the head and dashed for the back door, leaving Jo feeling rooted to the floor.

She couldn't be sure the black stallion was the same one she'd seen when the stage was held up—it had no distinctive markings—but there was no doubt about the paint. It had been ridden by the boy who had held out the pouch for her to drop her money and her locket into.

Her heart thudding, she watched as the bigger man dismounted, looped the reins over the hitching rail, and said something to his companion before heading across the street.

The remaining rider dismounted too, and a moment later, to Jo's total consternation, the boy headed straight to the front door of the Muddy Wells Mercantile.

6

Jo's mind raced. He would recognize her at once, and she would never be able to conceal the fact that she recognized him too, even though she had never seen anything of his face but his eyes.

He might not let her live long enough to testify against him. She had only seconds to consider what to do.

The display of hats was right beside her as she backed away from the window. The one she chose was not the pink-ribboned bonnet she had coveted, but the type of hat a widow might wear to her husband's funeral: plain, black, with a heavy veil to hide her anguish from the world.

It would cover her own features as well as anything she could devise on the spur of the moment. She barely had it settled on her head when she heard the door open.

What a horrid thing it would be to wear! She could see all right, actually, but through several thicknesses of heavy black netting everything was blurred.

Not so blurred that she wasn't certain about the boy, however.

He came in with a confident step, not even looking in her

direction until he had paused to give a thorough inspection to a pair of boots, elaborately tooled and expensive.

Jo's voice squeaked when she spoke. "Would you like to try them on, sir?

He jerked around to face her, and with his hat pushed back on his head that way, she could see his hair. Flaming, furiously red hair.

As if he knew she was looking at it, he pulled the Stetson firmly down over his forehead, though he couldn't possibly have seen her face through the veiling. "Oh, no, ma'am," he said hastily. "I couldn't afford them. No, I came in for this—"

He reached into the pocket of his plaid shirt and brought out a slip of paper to hand to her.

For a moment she couldn't make herself reach out for it. What if it was a note that said, "Hand over all your money or I'll kill you."?

He wasn't wearing a six-shooter, though. Trembling a little, Jo put out a hand and took the paper from him.

It was a shopping list. Sugar, coffee, beans, baking powder. Perfectly ordinary things.

Jo cleared her throat and tried to sound old enough to be a widow. "Yes, sir. I'll get these for you."

She knew where the coffee was, and the sugar. Beans were in a barrel, and she scooped them out into a bag and weighed them. Now where was the baking powder?

She wondered if the young bandit could hear her heart pounding. It sounded so loud she didn't even hear the door open again. The big man's voice startled her so that she turned sharply, hitting her elbow on the edge of the counter. Even the numbing pain was not as paralyzing as the fear that swept over her.

"Raisins," was what the man said. "Did you remember raisins?"

"No," the boy said. "We better have a couple of pounds of raisins, ma'am."

Jo's mind refused to function. Where would the raisins be? In another barrel, somewhere, but there were so many . . .

Where were Deputy Shaker and the judge? Where was someone to rescue her and arrest these men?

No one came, and she was still looking for the raisins. Flour, pickles, more beans, cornmeal, prunes—

Her mouth was almost too dry for speech. "I'm sorry, this is my first day here and I haven't located all the merchandise yet. I've found the prunes, but not the raisins—"

The big man interrupted impatiently. "Give us the prunes, never mind looking for raisins."

Jo measured out some of the prunes too, and steadied her voice with an effort. "Will that be cash or charge, sir?"

"Pay the lady, Rufus."

The boy's name was Rufus. That registered. So, automatically, did the details of his face: rather round, and with a sprinkling of freckles across a strong nose, with a wide, sensitive mouth that looked . . . kind.

What an odd thought. Why should she think that? He rode with a band of stage robbers; he had deprived her of the locket that was the only thing she'd had of value. He was *not* kind.

Jo began to add up the cost of the items, sliding a sideways glance at the big man. With no mask covering his face, he was revealed to be swarthy of skin, with thin lips and high cheekbones. Already, in the part of her mind that wasn't engrossed with adding up the cost of the groceries or praying that help would arrive, Jo noted the details for the drawing she would make of him: the heavy eyebrows, the pockmarks, the gap between his front teeth.

"Ma'am," said the boy called Rufus.

Jo jumped. "Yes?"

"The baking powder. I don't think we have that."

"Oh, yes." She looked around, wildly confused. "Oh, I didn't find it—"

"Up there. On the shelf right behind you," he said gently.

"Stop yapping and let's get out of here," the older man snapped.

"Be right with you, Slade," Rufus said, counting out the cash to pay the bill. He smiled at Jo. "Thank you, ma'am."

Slade, Jo thought. The big ugly one was Slade. Even if the lawmen didn't come in time, she would be able to provide them with excellent sketches and descriptions, and the men would be easier for the next posse to find.

She watched with mixed feelings as the pair left the store: relief that they were gone, regret that no one had showed up to arrest them. The coins in her hand were still warm from Rufus's touch when she dropped them into the cashbox.

Through the front windows she watched as Slade and Rufus remounted and rode away. Where in heaven's name were Andrew and the deputy?

It was a full ten minutes later, during which Jo debated whether or not she should lock up the store and run over to the saloon herself, before anyone showed up. The judge came briskly through the front door at almost the same moment as Deputy Shaker burst through the back one, gun drawn.

The deputy slid the six-gun back into his holster when he saw no one there but Jo. "I reckon we got here too late," he observed.

"I reckon you did, by a good quarter of an hour," Jo said,

sounding a bit sharp. "What took you so long? They were right here, two of them, and you could have captured them!"

"Fool at the door wouldn't let the boy in," the judge answered. "By the time we knew what he wanted, the rogues had already gone. What in tarnation are you got up for?"

At first Jo didn't know what he meant. Then the veil, which she had thrown back as soon as the bandits left, fell forward over her face. She reached up and took off the hat as her uncle said, "I don't think that one's quite your style."

"It was a disguise," Jo pointed out. "I didn't want them to know I was the one they robbed yesterday. If they knew I recognized them, what would they have done?"

"Quick thinking," Deputy Shaker approved. He reached for the sketch Jo had been making on the counter in front of her. "Got a good look at this one, eh?"

The judge stepped forward to see too. His eyes narrowed as he studied it. "Who taught you to draw like this?"

"Nobody. Grandma said it was a curse, because I was always drawing when she wanted me to be doing something else, like hanging out the wash or hauling water. Mama," Jo added, "said it was a gift from God."

The judge grunted, absorbing details from the sketch. "You say the other one called this one by name?"

"Slade," Jo confirmed.

"You didn't draw a picture of the second one?"

Jo felt a twinge of guilt, then wondered why. "I haven't had time yet. This one was obviously the leader; I thought it was more important to do him first."

"Did this Slade call the other one by name too?"

Why was she reluctant to say it? Jo only knew that she was. But with both men looking straight at her, waiting for her to speak, she had little choice. "Rufus," she said softly.

"Slade and Rufus," Deputy Shaker echoed. "Don't reckon I know of any desperadoes by those names. But you draw up a picture of this Rufus too young lady, and we'll get some wanted posters out. Couldn't anybody fail to recognize a face as ugly as this one. That Rufus, he ugly too?"

Jo swallowed. "No, sir. He's just . . . ordinary looking."

The judge put down the sketch and sighed. "Can you make a guess about their ages?"

Jo considered. "I reckon Slade's about the same age as Deputy Shaker."

"Thirty-six," the deputy said. "And how about Rufus?"

She was surer about that. "He wasn't full grown. Fifteen, maybe sixteen."

The judge nodded. "Well, I guess we better get back over to the courtroom and finish those trials, and decide when the hangings will be. You hold down the store, Josephine Eleanor Elizabeth Whitman, and get that other sketch drawn. We'll take over from there."

"They rode out of town to the west," Jo said. "Not hurrying or anything. They don't know anybody recognized them. Aren't you going to go after them?"

Deputy Shaker smiled. "Couple fellers already doing that," he told her. "Road only goes two ways, and we sent men both directions, just in case."

"But they don't know what the men look like!" Jo protested.

"True. But your little brother gave them a good description of the horses. One black stallion and a squatty little paint, right?"

"Right," Jo admitted. "Where is Andrew?"

"We told him to stay over at the saloon until we knew if there was one of them left over here. Didn't think so, because we didn't spot the horses, but no sense taking chances. We'll be back for that other picture, missy, after we get old Willy convicted and sentenced."

With that they headed out the front door and back across the street, leaving Jo, still feeling a little shaky in the knees, to write the bandits' purchases in the ledger.

When the door opened she jumped as if she'd been shot, but it was only the friendly Miss Susan Brown.

"Good morning," Miss Brown greeted her. "I dropped in to see if that new bolt of blue ribbon had come in yet. I need a couple of yards to renovate my best Sunday bonnet. My cat got hold of it and ruined the old ribbon, the pesky rascal."

But there was no blue ribbon. "Brown, green, black, and rose," Jo reported. "No blue. Perhaps you could use one of those."

"But it has blue flowers. No, I'd better wait till the new shipment of blue comes in." Miss Brown made a face. "I'll just have to make do with this one, though it isn't as pretty. And since this one clashes with my best blue dress, I won't be able to wear that, either."

She looked so downcast that Jo had a sudden intuition as to her reasons. Uncle Matthew had promised to bring Jo and Andrew to church, and Miss Brown wanted to look her best.

Impulsively, Jo turned to the display of ladies' bonnets, reaching over the one she'd used for a disguise to an exquisite natural straw with pale blue ribbons and white roses made of satin.

"Perhaps you might consider a *new* bonnet," she suggested, and handed it to her prospective customer. Grandma had always said that handling a coveted item was ill advised until one was prepared to buy it. Jo recalled something else Grandma had said about hats too.

"My grandma read the Bible every day. She knew it backward and forward. She told how Saint Paul ordered women to cover their heads when they went to church. He knew women take pride in their beautiful hair, and that looking at it could be distracting to the men, so he told them to cover it up. Only they fooled him, because they made their head coverings even more attention-getting than their natural hair. That tickled Grandma. She said a smart woman could outwit a man anytime if she set her mind to it."

Miss Brown had automatically taken the bonnet when Jo thrust it toward her, and was now looking at it more closely.

"This one is very pretty, isn't it?" she mused.

"Try it on," Jo urged, and reached for the mirror to show her how it looked.

So Miss Brown bought a new bonnet, and after that several other ladies came in to make small purchases, and an old cowpoke bought tobacco and rifle shells.

Andrew never did come back until the trial had ended. It was interesting to sit and watch the proceedings, and nobody chased him out. "They're going to hang him," Andrew reported. "I reckon they'll hang those others too, once they catch them," he concluded, looking longingly at the jar filled with licorice whips.

Jo felt an unpleasant knot at the pit of her stomach. She knew that desperadoes who preyed on honest citizens had to be punished, to be prevented from shooting more people or stealing their money or leaving them stranded without their horses so they died horribly of thirst or starvation. But somehow she had trouble dealing with the idea of the redheaded Rufus dangling from the end of a rope.

It was a thought that stayed with her after the judge came to take over the store and to purse his lips over the second sketch she had done. He didn't comment on it, only told her she could go on home and have some lunch and take Andrew with her.

"Only keep him away from the horses," he warned.

Jo and Andrew walked through the warm day, looking over the main street of Muddy Wells more carefully than they'd been able to do before, and Jo thought about the youngest of the bandits and wondered why he had turned to a life of crime.

By the time they reached the judge's house they were hot and sweaty and ready for a cold drink and some thick slabs of cold corn bread with sweet butter on it.

Jo welcomed the inner coolness of the house and reached for the dipper for a drink. When she made a little strangled sound of dismay, Andrew demanded, "What's the matter?"

Jo sounded hollow. "I forgot to put the maple syrup back down the well."

They both stared at the syrup jug in consternation.

It sat where she had left it, on the wooden table, and it was covered with ants.

Millions of ants. They came in a trail half an inch wide, through the doorway, across the floor, up a table leg, and up the side of the jug. They had also discovered the dirty dishes.

But that wasn't Jo's only shocking surprise.

When she ladled water over the first of the dishes to wash away the ants, she drew in an audible breath.

Inside the cup she hadn't even bothered to put into the dishpan lay proof that her disguise hadn't fooled the young bandit after all, and that he had been here, in this house, within the past few hours.

For within the cup, still stained with this morning's coffee, lay an object she had never thought to see again.

Her hand trembled as she fished it out and held it in her

palm: the locket with the precious pictures that the bandit called Slade had taken by force.

Jo felt light-headed, almost dizzy.

It wouldn't have been Slade who returned it, not after the way he'd taken it. No, it must have been Rufus, and he had discovered where she lived.

He must have made out her features in spite of the veil, or perhaps recognized her voice. Was he aware that she had recognized him as well?

Was he, she wondered with a surge of mingled excitement and fear, still here somewhere?

Andrew was behind her, chattering about the ants, but she scarcely heard him.

Her fingers closed around the locket and she dropped it into her pocket. She didn't know why she didn't tell her brother about it, but some inner voice warned her against it.

Instead she said, in a voice that sounded peculiar to herself but apparently aroused no suspicion in Andrew, "Come on. Help me clean up this mess. You can start by putting the syrup back down in the well, and bringing another bucket of water. We have to have the ants out of here before Uncle Matthew comes home and sees how stupid we were."

She concentrated hard on doing just that. Yet all the while the locket was there and her thoughts raced and guilt turned her face pinker than the heat could account for.

Would she, or would she not, tell the judge that for some reason the young bandit had returned her locket, and that he knew who she was, and where she was?

Perhaps, already, she knew the answer, and knew the judge would not approve of it.

7

Jo had supper ready to put on the table by the time the judge arrived. She had asked if she could bring home some white flour so that she could make biscuits for a change from the more common corn pone, and she'd searched the root cellar for potatoes, onions, turnips, and carrots to add to the remains of the roast Mrs. Bacon had cooked earlier for a savory stew.

She was proud of the meal and hoped her uncle would see that she could be an asset, not just a liability, by being here.

The judge walked in and hung up his hat, dipped tepid water into the basin, and washed his hands and face before he sat down. "Smells good," he offered, and Jo felt her cheeks warming at the suggestion of praise.

Andrew bowed his head as Jo took her own chair, and the judge drew back the fork that was about to spear a biscuit and waited for her to say the blessing.

She thought surely he would say something complimentary about the first mouthful of biscuit—she'd already sampled one to make sure they were as light and tasty as she'd hoped—but he didn't. Instead, he reached out to the edge of his plate and squashed an ant, and then, to Jo's horror, followed the line of tiny invaders across the table to the leg where they were climbing up from the floor.

"Forgot to put the syrup away this morning, eh?" he asked.

Jo turned red with embarrassment. "I scrubbed them all off, and even the floor! I didn't think they'd come back after that."

"Once they get the scent, they don't give up easy," her uncle said. "Put a saucer under each leg of the table and pour a little kerosene in each one. After a day or so they'll go looking somewhere else." He bit into another biscuit, dripping with melted butter, then started to laugh.

Jo stared at him, uncertain whether he was laughing at her or at something else.

"I remember one time I sneaked a hunk of Ma's gingerbread off to bed with me. Ate it in the dark, and didn't notice the crumbs falling around me. Guess I was about six years old. Anyway, I thought I'd got away with something, but"—he paused to butter another biscuit, sopping it in the gravy—"I woke up a while later thinking I'd sure enough gone to hell and the devil was punching me with a red-hot pitchfork! I started yelling and screaming, and Ma came in with the lamp. 'You ought to know better than to get cake crumbs in your own bed,' she told me. 'Drew every ant in the county.' They'd cleaned up most of the crumbs so they started on me. Ma dragged me out of bed and out by the rain barrel, and started throwing water over me to wash the ants off. It was November. Felt like I went from fire to ice. Ma said it served me right for taking what I'd been told I couldn't have." He shook his head and helped himself to more stew.

Jo hoped that meant he liked it, not just that he was starving hungry. She began to eat her own meal while there was still some left. She'd learned, living with Grandma, that a compliment to the cook was likely to result in more good cooking, but Uncle Matthew had apparently never thought that out.

The rest of the meal passed in silence until finally the judge pushed back his chair and looked Jo in the eye.

"The sheriff got some posters made up from those pictures you made. Stuck them up all over town. Sooner or later the bandits're going to show up again. In the meantime, how'd you like to be the bait to see if we can't get this Slade and Rufus to come in to us without sending another posse after them?"

"Bait?" Jo echoed, with the beginning of a prickle of apprehension. Bait was when you tied a goat out, helpless, so a tiger would come in and try to eat it. She'd read about that once. The idea was that a hunter would shoot the tiger while it was sneaking up on the goat, but Jo had shivered, imagining how the poor terrified goat must have felt.

Andrew was looking rather alarmed. "Jo isn't going to get hurt, is she?"

"No, no, of course not. But old Shaker and Sheriff Dalton and I are sort of hatching up a plan."

Jo waited, not liking the sound of being bait, not even to catch the stage robbers.

The judge didn't seem to notice her lack of immediate enthusiasm. "It just happens that day after tomorrow the stage from the west is going to be bringing in a fifty-two-pound gold nugget, on its way to the mint. We had us the bright idea of holding it over for twenty-four hours—got a good excuse, everybody knows our own stage driver was shot and not ready to drive again yet—and putting it into the safe at the Muddy Wells Mercantile. We're going to let the driver 'leak' that information out, and the word'll get around fast. Somebody like Slade, you can be sure he keeps his ear to the ground. He'll know about it. And," he concluded, "he'll make a try for it. Couldn't anybody like Slade pass up a chance for a fifty-two-pound gold nugget." He smiled with satisfaction.

Jo didn't smile. "Won't they realize it's a trap? I mean, a stage driver carrying that kind of a load would be risking his own life to talk about it."

"Oh, this driver's a smart enough fellow. We'll get him to do it in a way that won't arouse suspicion. Slade can't be all that smart, anyway, or he wouldn't still be around Muddy Wells after robbing that stage, taking a chance on being recognized. Particularly coming into the Mercantile with the boy after his hat got knocked off and the stage passengers saw he was red-headed, though I suppose he might not have noticed anybody saw that."

"Why won't he expect the nugget to be kept in the bank vault, then? That would be the safest place for something that valuable," Jo pointed out as a paralyzing dread crept through her.

"That's where we'll have to use our imaginations," the judge said. "We're going to let on that there's something wrong with the lock on that vault—that it's stuck shut and old Edderly—that's the president of the bank—has sent for an expert to get it open. He's even agreed to close down the bank for a day, supposedly waiting for the safecracker to come, to make it look legitimate. That leaves the safe at the Mercantile the only other logical place to put the nugget for safekeeping."

Jo's mouth was dry. "Where do I come in?"

"Well, we haven't made any secret of the fact that you drew the pictures for the wanted posters. So the gang isn't going to like you very much. The other thing, and the most important, is that you're going to be working at the Mercantile, while most of the men in town will be out with a posse, looking for Slade and his gang. They'll ride away with a lot of ruckus, make certain everybody in town knows what's going on, and head west. Supposedly we'll think nobody knows about the treasure in our safe, so we won't be worrying about that being unprotected while the men are somewhere else. There's just a chance Slade may try for the nugget in the daytime under those circumstances. What do you think about that?"

Jo swallowed. "It sounds . . . risky."

He was mildly annoyed. "Of course it's risky, but so is just sitting around waiting for them to strike again, when we don't know where they'll attack. If they're going after the nugget, they'll be coming to *us*, and we'll be ready for them."

While she recognized the logic of this, Jo thought there were a lot of things that could go wrong. Someone could easily get hurt. *Like me*, she thought, though she didn't say it.

Andrew's face was screwed up as he worked this through his mind. "But what's going to happen when the bandits come to the Mercantile to steal the nugget? What if they shoot Jo?"

"They won't. We'll have somebody waiting for them."

Jo sounded hollow. "I don't like that Slade, but I don't think he's as stupid as *you* think he is. I don't think he'll fall for a trap like that. Sir," she added, realizing how she had sounded.

The judge began to look hostile. The same way he'd looked when they got down off the stage and he'd realized one of his new charges was a female.

The sarcasm was heavy in his voice. "Oh. I suppose you could come up with a better plan."

Jo's mouth was dry. She didn't quite dare be totally frank. "Maybe," she said, swallowing.

"I see." He smiled again, but it wasn't exactly a friendly,

approving smile. "What would *you* do, Miss Josephine Eleanor Elizabeth Whitman?"

"Well," she said, "to begin with, I wouldn't set it up to have the stage driver let it be known there was an enormous gold nugget coming through Muddy Wells. Nobody but an idiot would believe he'd be so foolish, even if he was drunk."

She flinched at the expression on his face when she said the word *idiot*, and knew that she'd put it too forcefully.

"And so, instead, you would do . . . what?"

He was goading her, keeping his voice soft, but ready to crush her the moment she made a mistake. Jo knew that, hesitated, then swallowed once more.

"I'd have Andrew spread the story about the nugget being in the safe at the Mercantile, not a stage driver who ought to know better."

"I'd know better too!" Andrew interjected, frowning.

"Yes, of course, but the rest of the people in Muddy Wells don't know you. They'd be more likely to believe a nine-year-old boy would innocently reveal that he'd accidentally seen a huge nugget being put into the safe in his uncle's store, and didn't realize how important it was to keep it a secret, than that a grown man, and a stage driver used to carrying valuable cargo at that, would be so loose lipped. People would credit a little boy walking in just when the nugget was being transferred from the stage to the safe, overhearing his elders talking about how big it was, how valuable it was, and then scuttling out the back door without anyone knowing he'd seen it . . . so nobody would warn him to keep still about it . . . and then he talks to other boys, or one of the old codgers sitting in front of the hotel, spitting on the sidewalk . . . and within an hour everybody in

Muddy Wells knows about it. And *believes* the story without being suspicious."

The judge tapped his fingers on the table. His face was impassive. "And then what?"

Perhaps she had ought to shut up—Grandma had told her often enough that she didn't know when to close her mouth—but Jo couldn't stop now. If they intended to use *her* as part of the trap to catch the stage robbers, she was entitled to try to make the plot as safe for herself as possible. Having Slade and the others guessing that a trap had been set for them, and then figuring a way to outwit the law, seemed dangerous to her.

Jo drew in a deep breath and went on. "I'm not sure, except that if all the men in town go off with a posse, I should think *that* would make Slade suspicious enough to be wary."

The judge was scowling. "The men wouldn't *all* be gone. Naturally we would keep some of our best shots on guard, hidden at strategic places. The gang wouldn't be expecting that, but if most of the men in town are out with a posse they won't figure to get into a major gunfight, where they're evenly matched. They probably wouldn't show up in the daytime, either, but if they hear you're there—and know you can identify them and testify against them—they *might* try to get rid of you. That kind of thing has happened before. Or they might try to take you hostage until they can get away with the nugget. We wouldn't bring you into it if I thought it could really put you in any danger. We wouldn't even have to let them get all the way to the Mercantile, because once we've captured them your testimony would convict them of robbery whether they attempted to take the nugget or not. We'd have sharpshooters both sides of the Mercantile and try to take them before they got anywhere near you, but if they're keeping track, it's important they see you arriving at the store. Sort of an extra incentive."

Jo felt as if she were suffocating. She wished she shared his confidence that such a scheme was not dangerous. She stiffened when her uncle spoke again.

"It wouldn't bother you to coach your little brother in telling such a whopper? Or are you one of those people who believe the end justifies the means? Ma used to wash my mouth out with soap for lying or swearing."

"She also taught me that it wasn't always necessary to tell the *total, absolute* truth, like when Mrs. Farrell came to church in the ugliest hat we'd ever seen, and asked Grandma how she liked it. Mostly Grandma was so truthful it hurt, but that time she said the hat was 'handsome.' And I think, in order to capture a band of ruffians who go around robbing and threatening to shoot people, she'd agree that a little playacting would be all right. Andrew is good at playacting."

"Hmm." The judged studied her face thoughtfully. "You don't *look* like my sister Harriet, but you're certainly a lot like her. Bossiest female I ever knew."

And then, before Jo's indignation could spill out of her, he added, "But I'd have to say one thing about Harriet. In a pinch, she had some good ideas. One time I was caught in a flash flood when the creek climbed right out of its banks, and I thought I could ride a homemade raft across it. It got overturned and swept downstream, and Harriet ran ahead and cut across where that wide curve is, behind the barn. She let loose the brake on the wagon and got it going downhill so it landed across the creek just before I got there, screeching and swallowing water till I like to drowned. The wagon didn't go all the way across the creek, the way that water was swirling along, but

Harriet ran out onto the wagon and grabbed me by the hair and hauled me out. We had to float a ways before it wedged against the bank, and Ma never did understand how the wagon could have been swept away by the water when she'd parked it so close to the barn."

A small smile touched his mouth. "Once I got through choking and spouting up muddy creek water, I told Harriet if she'd been a few seconds later that blamed wagon could have come down right on top of me and drowned me for sure. And there she sat, all wet and muddy and having lost one of her shoes, and calmly told me she'd thought of that when she was shoving the wagon to get it started. Said she figured I'd either be killed or saved, and whichever it was to be was up to God. She was doing her best, but some things you have to take on faith that they're going to work, and that was one of them."

He shook his head slightly. "Yes, once in a while Harriet had a good idea. Well, all right, Miss Josephine Eleanor Elizabeth, we'll consider your way. Come into the parlor where the chairs are a little softer, and we'll talk about it."

Wondering what more there was to talk about, since she'd laid it out for him so plainly, Jo followed him into the parlor.

8

Now that she was committed to doing it, Jo was scared.

What if something went wrong? Slade and his gang members might not even hear the story about a gigantic gold nugget waiting in the safe at the Mercantile to be stolen. In that case, though the judge might become even more sour spirited, at least Jo would be safe.

Or, more likely, Slade might hear about it and guess that it was a trap. What if that were the case and he figured out some clever scheme to circumvent whatever the law was planning? What if he managed to get into the town and the store, perhaps disguised as . . . as a woman, or as a stooped old man, that no one would pay any attention to? What if he then shot Jo before he took the nugget and escaped altogether?

When she voiced her doubts, the judge snorted. "You sure do have an imagination," he said, which didn't make Jo feel a bit better.

After a little coaching, Andrew had gotten into the spirit of the whole thing. Together he and Jo had worked out the details of how he had supposedly sneaked into the Mercantile in the hope of getting a licorice whip without being noticed.

Everyone else was busy in the back room, he would say, and he had gotten not one but two of the black whips when he overheard part of a conversation in the storeroom where the men were putting something into the safe with great secrecy and many subdued exclamations.

Curious, Andrew was to relate, he had edged toward the doorway and learned what all the awestruck comment was about: a gigantic gold nugget that was being held for safekeeping until old Bill was able to take up the reins for the next stage run to the east. He had, Andrew would say, been disappointed that he hadn't actually seen the nugget, but since it would surely be in the safe for at least a day or two, he still had hopes of catching a glimpse of it. It wasn't as large as he'd expected, though, for it fit into a box only so big—and he'd gesture with his hands to show its size.

The judge, surprisingly, was the one who prompted him to mention that. Anyone who was knowledgeable about gold— and he suspected that could include the bandit Slade—might be convinced that the nugget was really there, a temptation he could not resist, if this detail were added.

Although the nugget had not yet arrived, and therefore Andrew could not actually view it, the judge gave him a convincing description of such a treasure in the probable words of those who *did* view it, and Andrew practiced so that no one was likely to doubt his story.

Andrew hadn't been in Muddy Wells long enough to make many friends—he'd only spoken to the two sons of Mr. Doane, the undertaker, after they'd thrown rocks at him while he was walking along Main Street. Andrew, lured by their giggles when they'd knocked his hat off, had pursued them into an alley and pelted them with a few rocks of his own. When he hit the little one with a stinging blow on the back of the head that sent the boy to his knees in the dust, and made him cry, Andrew apologized. He had been apologized to in return, and the boys had begun to be friends.

When it came time to actually tell the story, it seemed unlikely that the Doane boys, who were only seven and ten, could pass the news of a huge gold nugget along to the band of desperadoes who had robbed their father. So though Andrew told the boys—after swearing them to secrecy—about what he had supposedly seen at the Mercantile, he dared not let it rest there. Even if they broke their vows and repeated the information at home, it wasn't likely that Mr. Doane would relay such information in a casual fashion.

So Andrew sat down on the boardwalk in front of two elderly retired cowpokes resting in front of the hotel and eventually managed to get into a conversation with them while they spit tobacco juice past him into the street.

Life in Muddy Wells was not, for the most part, very exciting. Except for the stage robbery, which neither of the old men had actually seen, the most exciting thing they'd had to talk about in weeks was how amusing it had been when a wheel fell off a farmer's wagon a week ago and spilled the farmer and his wife into the street in a choking cloud of dust.

"You sure about that nugget, boy?" one of them asked, taking another chaw of tobacco. "They really said it weighed fifty-two *pounds?* Not ounces?"

Andrew nodded vigorously, and gestured with his hands as Jo watched him through the front window of the Mercantile across the street. Only moments later, the old men got up. One of them hobbled toward the saloon; the other headed for the blacksmith's, which was the other hub of social activity in town early in the day.

Jo's natural instinct in time of trouble was to say a prayer, but she didn't know how to word one this time. A part of her wanted to hope the whole idea would be a fiasco, that Slade and his gang would never hear the rumor about the nugget and so would never come looking for it while Jo was tending the store. Another part of her strongly wanted the men caught so that no one else need be subjected to robbery and being shot by these men.

And there was another factor in Jo's mixed feelings.

If the gang members were arrested and tried, they might well be sentenced to hang.

She kept seeing Rufus's face as she had drawn it: round, friendly-seeming with that smattering of freckles, the eyes bright and blue and seeing right through her disguise.

He had to be the one who had returned the locket with its precious pictures of her ma and pa. She wore it now, beneath her clothes so that no one would notice its return. She sighed and turned away from the window when Andrew got up and trailed after the old-timer who had headed for the blacksmith's. A boy could hang around there and listen if he liked, without being chased away, where he wouldn't have been allowed inside the saloon.

Why did Rufus return the locket? Jo asked herself as she began to stack cans of peaches on one end of the counter where the housewives would be enticed by them.

There was only one answer she could think of: He hadn't really wanted to take her locket, when she'd begged him to let her keep at least the pictures. If Slade hadn't lashed out with that six-gun, she was sure the young bandit would have allowed her to retain the pictures.

Yet he hadn't returned only those, but the locket itself. It was made of gold and intricately embossed, so it was valuable.

Rufus must have been sorry for her. Maybe he'd even liked her a little bit.

Nobody had ever really liked Jo before. Not a *boy*. Oh, the Swanson twins, Richard and Ian, had pulled her hair and tripped her when the young people were playing around the churchyard at the evening services. Grandma said that was a boy's peculiar way of showing her attention, because they thought she was interesting. It seemed a stupid way, to Jo, because it had exasperated her rather than excited her own interest in return.

The Swansons had stolen her sandwiches at school, played keep-away with her apple, and drawn crazy pictures of her on their slates when they were supposed to be doing their sums. Jo had failed to feel appreciative about any of these things.

The boy named Rufus was different.

She liked his looks, and she *did* appreciate his returning her locket. The fact that he was a member of a gang of stage robbers bothered her a lot, but as she placed the last can of peaches on top of the stack, Jo knew that she would hate to see Rufus caught and punished with the others.

Perhaps that was why she hadn't told anyone about the return of the locket.

She knew the judge would be angry to learn that one of the bandits had actually entered his house, even in order to return Jo's trinket. And she didn't want to cause any more friction between them than already existed, though her uncle was turning out to be less of a menace than she had thought at first.

Of course there was the matter of being the bait to lure Slade's gang to town so they could be captured. The judge was enthusiastic about that, and she'd swallowed hard and agreed to be the "goat," but she wasn't as sure as he was that it was all going to turn out quite as perfectly as he assumed.

She rather liked working in the Mercantile, except for thinking about what it would be like to face Slade when he turned up. She was meeting practically everybody in Muddy Wells, for sooner or later everyone needed something that only Uncle Matthew kept on his shelves.

The women had been friendly, and a girl near her own age who had been in had told her about an upcoming ice-cream social and a Sunday school picnic to which she was cordially invited.

She kept watching for a rather slight figure with flaming red hair, perhaps covered with a hat, but there was no sign of Rufus nor any of his companions. She saw none of the horses belonging to the bandits, either, as she watched through the front windows while putting up cans and boxes or waiting on customers.

It was late in the day when the judge came across from the hotel where he'd been on unexplained business. He was carrying a letter, which he dropped onto the counter where Jo was measuring off six yards of checked gingham for Mrs. Hilson, who wanted to rehash the stage robbery in great detail.

That only made Jo more nervous, and she was glad to hand over the goods. "Six yards at eleven cents a yard. That'll be sixty-six cents," she said, accepting the lady's payment and making change. Mrs. Hilson reluctantly took her leave after a sideways glance at the judge.

"This appears to be for you as well as for me," the judge said, viewing the unopened missive as if it might be a rattlesnake that would strike if he continued to hold it.

"Oh?" Jo bent over to look at it more closely. "Oh, from Aunt Harriet."

It seemed strange to see her own name written on a letter. She couldn't recall that she'd ever had a letter of her own before, even if this one also was addressed to Judge Matthew Macklin, Muddy Wells, Texas.

It appeared that *he* wasn't going to open it, so Jo did, spreading it flat on the counter to read it.

It was dated two weeks earlier, in Galveston, and was written in Aunt Harriet's bold, strong hand.

"Dear Matthew and children," Jo read aloud. "By the time this arrives Jo and Andrew will undoubtedly have arrived in Muddy Wells. I know you are ill equipped to care for youngsters, Brother—in fact, I fear for their upbringing if they are entrusted to your care for any length of time—"

The judge snorted, but Jo kept on reading.

"—so I assure you I will make all haste to travel to Huntsville to take over Ma's holdings as soon as it is possible. As you know, I lost my husband Travis some months previous, poor soul, and I have no ties to keep me here once I have disposed of the property Travis bought for our family. I have always been uneasy in my present surroundings, due mainly to my aversion for hurricanes along the coast. I have sorely missed my home in the Piney Woods for all the years I've been gone from it. Since Ma disowned me for marrying Travis, and she would not have welcomed us home as a couple, I did not feel I could return until now. She was, perhaps, right about Travis's inability to earn a proper living for a family, for his luck ran consistently to the unfortunate, but I assure you he was a man of good humor and pleasant temperament, with few bad habits, and I in no way regret having wed him.

"However, as a widow with three children to support—the new baby is a girl, as I had prayed for—I'm sure I'll be best off in Ma's old house, and then Josephine and Andrew will be able to finish their growing years in familiar surroundings, in a woman's care."

The judge snorted again, though he had certainly expressed a reluctance to take them even temporarily himself.

"This is to inform you, therefore, that within a few months I hope to have settled up my affairs here. With most people still struggling to make up for what they lost during the war, and with so few having any significant amount of cash, it may take a little time to sell our cabin and the land inherited from my father-in-law. One neighbor has expressed an interest. If nothing else happens between now and when he is able to ship his current cotton crop, the price of it may enable him to pay the modest price I am asking for my place. I must have enough so that I can pay off our remaining debts and have a new tongue put on the wagon, and it's in need of a new wheel as well before I would dare to venture on such a journey. I will be bringing my family to Huntsville in the wagon carrying our household goods. Once I've arrived, I will send a telegram notifying you of that fact, and you can put the children on a stage to come home. It is indeed a pity that no one in Huntsville could be found to keep the children until I could leave here, but be assured that I will do my best to take over responsibility for them before the summer is done."

Jo's heart leaped in anticipation at the thought of going home, and then she wondered why there was also a thread of regret through her reflections. She cleared her throat and continued.

"Since you are undoubtedly in a better financial state than I, Matthew, I trust that your familial spirit will lead you to cover the cost of their travel. It would also be generous of you, and appropriate, to make a contribution to your widowed sister's establishment of a new home for all these orphaned and half-orphaned children."

Jo slid a sideways glance at her uncle, to see the judge rolling his eyes heavenward. She pretended not to notice.

"There will, of course," Aunt Harriet went on, "have to be additions made to the house to accommodate the lot of us. I am in hopes that a workman may be hired locally to take care of that, which means I'll need funds to pay him. As I'll be arriving before winter, God willing, the children may all sleep out in the yard for a few months while the building is accomplished.

"I do hope, Matthew, that you are taking your responsibilities as an uncle seriously. Ma would want them to continue to attend Sunday school, for instance. And to eat regular meals, with more variety than the pot of beans I suspect is your usual fare six days of the week. Also, remember that children must be supervised and disciplined when necessary, though the last must be tempered by affection. Failing that, unaccustomed as you may be in this regard, at least try to be reasonable.

"To Josephine and Andrew, I send affectionate greetings and pray that you will be obedient and respectful of your elders at all times.

"As ever, your sister and aunt, Harriet Unwin."

In the silence as Jo fell quiet the judge groaned. "You see? That's the way she talked to me when I was Andrew's age."

"Didn't she like you?" Andrew asked, puzzled.

"Not very much. Especially," the judge added, humor replacing irritation, "after I left the toad in her bed when she was eleven. For days afterward she examined her body closely every day, looking for the warts she was sure would appear."

Jo looked at him reservedly. "No wonder she didn't like you."

"Oh well. I'm glad I'm not the one who has to live with her. I'd rather send her the money than have to do that. And we aren't doing so badly so far, are we?"

"We're doing great," Andrew told him, having been promised that after supper that night he could again ride Jury.

Jo didn't comment. She wondered what Aunt Harriet would think of the judge using her as bait for his trap to capture the Slade gang, and her uneasiness grew and grew until she felt half sick with it.

9

Jo had been in bed for quite a long time, but had not fallen asleep. The locket was hot against her skin; it made her remember the warmth in the coins she had taken from the young bandit's hand. And that made her think of Rufus himself.

He looked like any nice, ordinary boy. She had been frightened of him when the stage was held up, because he wore a bandanna tied over his face and had been the one passing around the pouch for the passengers' valuables.

He would not have insisted on taking pictures and all, she was convinced, if it hadn't been for Slade. And he had brought the locket back to her, taking considerable risk to do so, for if he'd been caught the penalties would be severe.

Why had he done that? And what would Slade do if he found out the boy had returned some of the loot? Unlike the cash, the locket was distinctive enough to be missed.

The night was hot and still, and she threw back the sheet, which had become tangled around her. It got hot in the Piney Woods too, but she couldn't remember very many nights that had stayed as bad as this, when sweat made her nightgown stick to her skin and she felt as if she were trying to breathe heated air right off the top of a roaring stove.

Jo sat up and slid out of bed. Across the hall, Andrew apparently slept peacefully, unaware of the misery of a summer night in Muddy Wells. The little ones could sleep through anything, Grandma had always said; it was only when you grew up that such things as the weather bothered you.

Thinking of Grandma, missing her so much, Jo felt her eyes prickle. She tried to decide if it would help enough to be worthwhile if she went downstairs for a basin of water and had herself another sponge bath. Maybe she could fall asleep before that little dab of coolness wore off again.

In the night silence she heard crickets chirping, and then there was another sound. Hoofbeats, coming fast. Out by the barn, the dogs began to bark.

She bit her lip. If company came she wouldn't be able to go downstairs for the water until after they'd gone. It was already too late to get it before whoever it was arrived, unless she got fully dressed again.

She rose and went to the window, hoping to be able to tell who was coming. The night was too dark; even when the rider reached the yard, she couldn't make out his identity. The hounds recognized him, though, with a few yaps of welcome and ran to meet him.

Not a breath of air stirred, though she could smell the dust that rose as the rider reined in below. She even thought she could tell when the grit of it settled on her skin, and she longed for home. Back at Grandma's house, she would have walked out the door and down to the creek, where the cooling water would have been just right, this time of year, for bathing. In Muddy Wells there was no creek worth mentioning; since she'd been here it was so shallow she could practically walk across it with her shoes on and not get much more than the soles wet.

Before the rider could knock, the door opened and the

lamplight spilled out into the yard. Jo craned her neck. The rider was already up on the porch so she couldn't see him, but she recognized his voice immediately.

"Evening, Judge." It was Deputy Shaker. "I thought you'd want to know the news before it comes out next week in the *Gazette*. Been another bank robbery, over to Dry Creek Station."

The judge's voice was crisp. "Same gang? Slade?"

"Sure sounds like it, except there was only four of them, not five. Two witnesses saw them, described the horses. One of them was a big black. They shot old Trudell when he refused to open up the safe."

"Dead?" the judge asked.

"'Fraid so. Broad daylight, mind you. Bank was just closing up, so there weren't any customers, but there were people on the street. Cleaned out the vault. Oh, something interesting."

Jo leaned out the open window, straining to hear every word. Her heart was pounding. Only four bandits, not five. Who was missing? Was Rufus among them or not? She knew it didn't matter who did the actual shooting of the man named Trudell; all the others who were in on the robbery were just as guilty as the shooter, and this time the charge would be murder.

Oh, please God, Jo thought, let it be Rufus who wasn't there. They'd hang him for certain.

"Sheriff at Dry Creek asked me was it true, we got a seventy-pound nugget in the safe at the Mercantile."

There was small silence. Jo pictured her uncle smiling a little.

"Guess the story is getting around, then. What did you tell him?"

"Told him it weren't but fifty-two pounds, not seventy, and to keep his mouth shut about it."

"Good. Good," the judge said. "I'm sorry about old Trudell. He was a decent enough sort, for a banker. Well, if the story young Andrew told got all the way to Dry Creek this fast, I'd say it's likely Slade and his men have heard it too. It was a good idea the girl had, more convincing than if a stage driver got drunk and talked too much. This scheme better work, Shaker. People are getting pretty riled up, the way the stages and the banks are being held up, and people being shot."

"For certain," the deputy agreed, even as Jo swallowed hard against her uncle's words. *The girl*, he'd called her. Why couldn't he think of her as enough of a real person to call her by her name?

"Oh, by the way," Deputy Shaker said. "Old Bill's feeling a lot better. Expects to be able to take the stage out as soon as we want to move that nugget. He said he's well enough now to join us covering the Mercantile while young Jo minds the store. One more gun when those bandits show up."

"We can't let anything happen to her," the judge said firmly. "Have to be enough of us around to make sure she's safe."

"We'll take care of Jo," the deputy said, and the conviction in his voice made her feel a little better. So did the fact that the judge cared about her safety, even if he couldn't act as if he liked her enough to use her name instead of calling her *girl*.

Jo stood there until the men had concluded their conversation and the deputy had ridden off. She no longer felt like going downstairs for water to bathe. She went back to bed and lay there for some time longer, thinking how scary it was, baiting the trap. And thinking as well about Rufus, wondering if he was no longer with the gang, wondering if maybe something awful had happened to him.

He might have been shot during the commission of another robbery, though she thought if anyone in the county had shot him at such a time someone would know about it. No, more likely—

Jo drew in a deeper breath and for a moment lay rigid.

What if Slade realized Rufus had returned the locket, and had been so angry he killed him?

No, no, surely not, she thought desperately. But then where was Rufus? She didn't know why she was so sure that the boy was the one who had *not* been with the gang that robbed the Dry Creek Station bank, except that it was what she wanted to believe.

And when Slade's band came to steal the huge nugget while she was tending the store, she prayed that Rufus would not be with them.

It was a long time before she could sleep, and even then her slumber was filled with disturbing dreams.

She woke early, and already, though the sun was barely above the horizon, it was sickeningly hot. She wished she could dress like Andrew, in only a pair of loose overalls, with no underwear.

Instead, of course, being female, she had to wear all those undergarments and a dress that covered her from throat to toes, though she left the top couple of buttons undone, at least until it was time to go to the store.

In spite of the heat, she felt a chill too. No sense trying to tell herself that nothing could go wrong if the Slade gang came today; nobody could predict what Slade would do. The judge had said he probably wouldn't come into town in the daytime, and he was probably right. Slade would be a fool, really, to think he could walk into the Muddy Wells Mercantile and get into the safe for the enormous nugget, then simply ride away with it.

Slade was mean and treacherous, but he wasn't stupid. At least not *that* stupid, though of course being a bandit in the first place wasn't exactly intelligent.

At any rate, she was afraid of him. Afraid of what might happen today if the plot worked and Slade was drawn to that nugget as expected. She paused for a moment, feeling the heat that lingered from the previous day in the boards beneath her bare feet, and offered a quick prayer: If they come, please let them be intercepted before they get as far as the Mercantile.

Her fingers fumbled over her buttons, and the dampness of her skin was not entirely due to the early morning heat. She paused before her brother's room on her way downstairs. His door had been left open, as had her own, for cross-ventilation, though there was no hint of a breeze. Andrew lay atop the sheets, still sound asleep.

Jo moved silently on the stairs. Below them, the judge's door was closed. He might not awaken for another hour, she thought, as the grandfather clock in the parlor struck six.

The kitchen was neat, as she had left it last night, with the table already set for breakfast. The coal oil in the saucers had done the job, and there were no ants on the clean plates. The idea of starting a fire in the stove to cook anything made her stomach curdle, and she wondered if her uncle would settle for something cold, like a chunk of corn bread. Andrew would, he'd eat anything.

Of course the judge liked coffee in the morning. There was no way to get coffee without building a fire that would heat the kitchen past the point of being bearable.

Jo sighed and let herself out onto the back porch, easing the screened door quietly closed so as not to rouse the sleepers.

Outside it was a bit cooler, and she took a deep breath, filling her lungs, remembering similar dawns back in the Piney Woods. Remembering the days when Mama was still alive, when Grandma would have been giving orders about the day, when what she'd had to look forward to was her usual chores and then free time to wade in the creek, or gather wildflowers scattered through the woods for bouquets to brighten up the house. Or, best of all, to sit quietly beneath a tree sketching the squirrels that would have been watching her from an overhead limb.

When she hadn't had such a queer, stomach-tightening tremor running through her at the thought of having to face a brutal bandit one more time.

Jo picked up the basket from the porch rail and headed for the henhouse. She'd gather the eggs and scatter corn for the chickens, always keeping a sharp eye out for old Rusty, the rooster, whose habit it was to sneak up behind a person and attack her legs.

For all her care, though, Rusty surprised her. She had bent over to pick up the seventh egg when the rooster struck her exposed ankles.

Jo gave a yelp of pain and fury, nearly breaking the egg by squeezing it too hard as she turned to defend herself. "If you belonged to me," she told the beady-eyed Rusty, "I'd wring your neck and have you for Sunday dinner, with dumplings."

The rooster squawked and made another run at her, but this time her skirts covered her ankles and he didn't manage to touch her.

Jo was still muttering under her breath as she filled the

basket and left the henhouse. Even nice fresh eggs held no appeal this morning, since they'd have to be cooked to be eaten.

If she ate anything, Jo suddenly thought, she might not be able to keep it down. No doubt the judge would think that absurd, but then *he* wasn't going to be the bait, along with the nugget, for drawing in a killer.

She was halfway across the yard toward the house when a horse whinnied, and there was the sound of something bumping against the wall, or falling, inside the barn.

Jo stopped. The horse whinnied again. She didn't think any of the horses were kept in the barn. They were either in the corral or in the fenced pasture beyond it.

If there was a reason why a horse had been put into the barn, the judge wouldn't necessarily have told her. Maybe she'd better see if there was something wrong, she decided uneasily, though she didn't see how a horse could get into trouble unless someone had neglected to secure his stall door. If he were loose in there, he might have knocked the lid off the oats barrel, and if he gorged on those, he could wind up with an awful bellyache.

Carrying the egg basket over one arm, she approached the barn. The door on the end was open, and she stepped into the dim interior, smelling dust and hay and horse manure.

Something moved in the deeper shadows.

Not a horse, it was too small for that.

Fear suddenly gripped her. Jo halted, feeling the warmth of the sun on her back, the coolness inside the barn. She knew she was silhouetted against the light; if it was a person in there, he could see her even though she couldn't see him.

Him. Who? Slade?

No, it wouldn't be Slade skulking around in a barn. That wouldn't be his style. Not at dawn, anyway.

She couldn't think what to do. She just stood there, and

then a big yellow cat emerged from the darkness, yowling as it twined around her feet, and Jo gave a shaky laugh.

"Was that you?" Certainly the cat didn't appear to be alarmed, only hungry. "Well, *you* wouldn't have uncovered the oat barrel, would you? Maybe I'd better look, just in case. Uncle Matthew wouldn't want the rats to get into it, even if his horse couldn't reach it."

She remembered where the barrel was. Halfway down, to the right of the open space between the stalls on one side and the hay storage area on the other. Against one of the supporting posts, which she could make out now that she'd stepped completely out of the sunshine.

The cover *was* off the barrel.

There was no sign of rats, and the horse whinnied again in the corral just as Jo's foot encountered the barrel lid.

With no warning a hand closed over her mouth from behind and held her fast, while a low voice warned, "Don't yell."

Her heart swelled in her chest and the earlier apprehension became panic as the strong fingers partially cut off her breathing.

Jo froze and waited for whatever was to happen next.

10

Jo was aware of dust motes swirling in the stray band of sunlight that came through the open doorway, of the cat still yowling softly for something to eat, of the hound giving her rigid hand a friendly lick.

Greeting her, yes, and seeming not at all alarmed about whoever else was in the barn.

"Shh!" her captor cautioned. "I'm going to take my hand away, but don't scream, all right?"

She knew the voice, and the fear diminished, but her heart was still racing. When he released her, Jo turned slowly to face the redheaded bandit.

Not that she could see his hair; it was covered by a worn, dusty hat. And even though his back was to the open door through which the sunlight poured, and thus in shadow, she could see his face. It caused her to suck in a breath of consternation.

"What happened to you?"

She had never before seen such ugly bruising. The boy's lips were swollen and discolored, and there was a livid reddish-purple weal on one temple as well as one over the opposite cheekbone.

Rufus didn't reply, and Jo came to her own conclusion. "Slade?"

Clearly it hurt when he spoke; his lips were stiff, and cracked when he attempted a smile. "He doesn't like it when anybody crosses him."

"You brought back my locket."

"Pictures of your ma and pa inside, weren't they? I don't have any picture of *my* folks, but I figured they were important to you. I reckon girls set a lot of store by such things."

"Yes," Jo agreed softly. Her heart was beginning to slow its mad pace, but she was still filled with tension. One of the hounds licked her hand again, and she looked down at him with disgust. "Some watchdog you are," she accused.

Rufus grinned, then put a hand to the place where his lip was split and spoke through his fingers. "I brought 'em each a nice chunk of roasted rabbit when I came before. They were looking for more this time, but I didn't have time to get me a jackrabbit and cook it, not with Slade on my tail."

"He was chasing you?" Jo shifted the basket of eggs to the other arm because they were getting heavy.

"Well, he didn't have me in sight. But I figured if I didn't keep moving he'd catch up with me soon enough. He doesn't want me running loose, I expect, and he was sure enough in a bad mood when he found out the locket was missing. I told him I lost it, but he guessed I'd given it back."

His face was proof of that. Jo swallowed, imagining how it would feel to have one's flesh pounded that way. Grandma had switched her legs a time or two when she was little, for some misdeed like running away to play in the creek when she was supposed to be taking a nap, or for eating a bucket of berries Grandma had painstakingly picked for jam. But no one had ever struck her in such a way as to leave marks like these.

"Is he your pa?" It was suddenly very important that this not be the case. It would be terrible to have a pa like Slade.

Rufus turned now so that more of the light fell on his face, and the damage done to it was even more apparent. Jo bit her lip, appalled, almost aching herself, just looking at it.

"No," Rufus said with vehemence. "He's only my step-pa, and now that Ma's dead, I don't reckon he's even that anymore."

"Will he come after you, then? What will he do if he finds you?"

Again he smothered the wry impulse to laugh, because laughing hurt lips that had been split by a man's knuckles. "Well, I'm in hopes of not seeing him again. Trouble is, I was riding like a wild man, trying to get far enough way so he couldn't find me, and poor Comanche stepped in a hole. Threw me onto the rocks, and I hurt my arm"—she noticed now that he was holding his left arm still, close to his body—"and by the time I pulled myself together, he'd gone galloping off and I couldn't catch him. So I was afoot, and I didn't know where to go or what to do. I had some grub in my saddlebags, but that was gone too, and my stomach so empty it thinks my throat's been cut."

He looked sheepish. "I remembered there were horses here, in the corral, when I came to leave the locket. I figured there'd be oats too, maybe. Not so tasty, raw, but better than nothing."

Jo had never felt anything like the fluttering that was going on in her stomach. She was scared, and excited, and something else she couldn't quite put a name to.

"How did you know where to find me?"

Rufus shrugged. "Not much of a problem in a town the

size of Muddy Wells. Everybody knows everything about everybody else. And they all talk about it. We came to town for supplies right after the stage robbery, and everybody was talking about that. They talked about you too. Judge Macklin's niece that had come to stay for a while. The livery stable had a couple of the judge's horses over there. All we had to do was stand around and listen, and somebody mentioned the judge's house. Fine house, they said, and a nice piece of land on the edge of town, and he planned it all for some lady run off with a traveling salesman or some such. They wondered how the judge would take to having a young female relative come to stay. They said enough about his place so it wasn't hard to figure out which one it was, when you can stand on the hill and see every house in town all at the same time. And then when I got there to his gate, his name's on it, plain as anything to one who can read. My ma taught me to read."

There were plenty older than he was who couldn't, so he had a right to be proud of that. "Slade admired the horses and asked if they might be for sale. Livery man said Judge Macklin was a regular expert on good horseflesh and wasn't much for selling any of his except for a real good price. I recognized the horses later, here."

"And you were going to steal one of them." Jo kept her voice carefully under control, trying not to sound accusing.

"Well, I thought about it," Rufus admitted. "But I figured stealing a horse from a judge was a pretty poor idea. And up to now I never stole anything except what Slade *made* me steal. I never set out to be any thief, and I know it would break Ma's heart if she knew I was one."

Jo was silent, digesting that. She'd sure have hated to have Slade for a stepfather. And then she remembered the bank robbery.

She moistened her lips. "Were you with the rest of the gang when they robbed the bank over at Dry Creek Station?"

She could tell from his face that he hadn't known about it. Not unless he was an awfully good actor. "When?" he asked, sounding hoarse.

"Yesterday. Just before closing time. They shot and killed the president of the bank."

For a brief moment, Rufus closed his eyes, as if to shut out the reality. His chest rose and fell as he drew in a deep breath and let it out.

"No. I wasn't there. No way I can prove it, though. I was hiding out in the cottonwoods along the stream until it got dark enough so I could get in here. I *did* swipe some oats. I was going to move on before dawn, but I guess I overslept." His blue eyes bored steadily into hers. "You going to call your uncle and turn me in?"

Jo had been wrestling with that from the moment she realized he was there. "If I turn you in," she said softly, "they'll try you along with the others, when they get them. For the stage robbery if not for the bank and shooting the banker."

Rufus looked pale under the tanned skin. "And I expect they intend to hang the lot of us."

Jo's throat closed, and she couldn't reply to that. She didn't need to. After a moment, when the worst of the ache had begun to subside, she said, "How long have you been riding with Slade and his gang?"

Rufus pushed back his hat with his good hand, so that the sun slanting in through the barn door struck the coppery-colored hair. "He never made me do it until after Ma died. That's seven months ago." He cleared his throat. "Ma was a schoolteacher. My own pa was a farmer, and I had a little sister, Hildy. We had our own place, with horses and chickens and a cow and everything. It was hard work for everybody, but I liked it. Our farm was kind of like this one of your uncle's, except we had more fields where we raised corn and hay and oats, and all our own vegetables. Then Pa went off to the war." He had to clear his throat again. "He was killed, and Hildy got sick and died. She was only eight. That left Ma and me to run the farm, and it was awful hard. So when Tom Slade came along, home from the war, and he was nice to Ma, she finally gave in and married him."

The unhappiness in his face twisted Jo's heart. "I never liked him, really. I couldn't believe Ma did, either, but he was nicer to her than he was to me. And she thought we needed a man on the place. I reckon she knew it was a mistake before very long, but there wasn't much she could do about it then. He stopped being so nice to her, and he sold off everything but the house and the barn. Got rid of all the farming land. He was no farmer. He wanted a living without working for it. He didn't say where he went or what he did, but he always had money."

He turned away, looking out into the sun-washed barnyard where the heat was already increasing, though the sun had risen only a little way in the eastern sky. Jo wondered if there were really tears glistening on his eyelashes, or if she only imagined it.

"I figured he was stealing somewhere, and I guess Ma did too, but she was afraid of him by that time. The one time she challenged him, he hit her." His mouth was a hard, flat line. "I wanted to kill him for that, but I didn't dare. Then Ma got sick and died, and I reckon she went to heaven to be with Pa. But I was left with Tom Slade. In as close to hell as it can get on earth."

Jo remembered how Slade had struck out at Rufus, forcing

him to collect the stage passengers' valuables, and she believed him. Even without the evidence of his battered face.

"What are you going to do now?" she asked gently.

Rufus continued to stare out the barn door. "Keep running, I guess. Until I get far enough away so nobody ever heard of Tom Slade or his gang."

"With no money? No food? You don't even have a gun to shoot rabbits to eat, do you?"

He made a snorting sound. "Slade didn't trust me with a gun. Maybe he knew how I itched to turn one on him, march him to a sheriff's office, and turn him in."

"So how will you live, if you don't steal?"

He ran his tongue over his lips, wincing when he came to a scab that had cracked open at the corner of his mouth. "Find me a job, I reckon. I can work. I'm sixteen, near a man. And I'm strong. Only I need to get a long way from Muddy Wells or any other place Slade might come along. He doesn't take kindly to anybody who defies him; and after he beat me up, I knew I wasn't sticking around for more. Either beating or robbing. It would help if I had a horse, but I don't know where old Comanche went. I thought I'd head back out to where I lost him, but more'n likely he went home, and I don't dare go there."

There was such discouragement in his voice that Jo felt the prickle of tears. She'd lost her family too, except for Andrew, but at least she'd been sent to live with the judge, not with a bullying bandit like Slade.

"Maybe," she said tentatively, "Slade's gang will be caught. There are a lot of armed men looking for them. Then, if they're locked up, it would be safe for you to travel. To find a job."

Rufus sighed. "Yeah. Only he's still out there, and I've got an empty belly." He glanced hopefully at the basket of eggs on her arm. "I don't suppose you could spare me a couple of those."

"Raw?" Jo asked.

"Raw eggs won't kill you. My old dog used to eat them." His mouth twisted. "Before Slade kicked him to death for tripping him. I could stir them up with some of those oats; they probably wouldn't be too bad tasting."

Jo picked an egg out of the basket and handed it over, then a second one. "There's cold corn bread in the house."

Rufus grinned as best he could with that swollen mouth. "Makes my mouth water," he told her. "I'd be obliged, ma'am. Then all I have to do is figure out where to hide out until I can get away."

Jo remembered the sketches she had made of him, which were now posted all over town. "The judge . . . probably wouldn't understand, that Slade made you do things you didn't want to do."

"Probably not," Rufus agreed. "Oh, oh!"

He stepped quickly away from the door, deeper into the shadows, as a shout came from the house.

"Jo? You out there?"

Her heart suddenly pounding as if the judge had just walked in on them, Jo emerged from the barn and called back. "Here, I'm getting the eggs! I'll be in to get breakfast right away!"

The judge stood on the back steps, shading his eyes against the sun that promised to produce egg-frying temperatures before noon. "Never mind cooking, it's too blamed hot to light the stove. We'll eat in town, and we've got a big day ahead! Come in and get ready to go."

Behind her, in the gloom of the barn, Rufus echoed, "A big day? Something special going on?"

She didn't look back at him. The judge might wonder why. Jo bent over as if to retrieve something, so her uncle couldn't possibly tell she was speaking, and said in a low voice, "The judge never locks the door. Go in and get the corn bread—it's wrapped in a towel on the lower shelf. There's butter down the well."

She dared not take time for more. Walking briskly toward the house, she felt perspiration breaking out all over, and part of it was from anxiety. Over the day ahead, over what would happen to Rufus if the judge discovered the fugitive in his barn.

Rufus didn't deserve to have to go to trial with the others, Jo thought. But would the judge or the sheriff see that? And if they arrested him, would he be sentenced to jail or to be executed, the same as the others?

Entering the house, she groped in her pocket for a handkerchief to wipe the moisture from her face, and said a brief prayer before she faced her uncle.

Please, God, help me to know what to do.

She remembered when she had asked God to strike the robbers dead, and He had not complied. Her hands were trembling as she put the basket of eggs on the table and went to tidy her hair before they left for the Mercantile. To wait and see if Slade and his gang went for the bait of the golden nugget. To worry about what he might do if he realized that the sheriff and the judge had set a trap for him.

In spite of the heat, Jo felt a chill. She wished she had never agreed to be part of what could be a very dangerous plan to capture the bandits.

And over it all, she felt heartsick that there was nothing she could think of to do to save Rufus.

11

The day was long and tense.

Shortly after Jo arrived at the store, the posse assembled in front of the sheriff's office. She watched them through the window of the Mercantile, peering over a display of ladies' gloves and bolts of blue checked gingham and flowered calico.

The men were of all ages, most of them clearly excited, a few of the older ones grim jawed. They didn't know this was a wild goose chase, that the "sighting" of the bandits was a bit of fiction on the part of Deputy Shaker, and that there was no reason to think Slade and his gang had been anywhere near the area where they believed they were going to pursue him.

Deputy Shaker, in an attempt to be more convincing in his excuse for staying behind, had gotten quite imaginative. He had ridden into town an hour earlier, clutching one shoulder, which he had liberally soaked in chicken blood, claiming to have been ambushed by the notorious gang. Pushing past the spectators who had materialized from the blacksmith shop, the saloon, and the streets, the deputy had vanished into the little office where Doc Scobie was supposedly patching him up.

Shortly thereafter, the drama continued to unfold. Sheriff

Dalton himself, summoned by a small boy who had stood around wide-eyed as Deputy Shaker was assisted off his horse, had emerged from Doc's office and issued a call for volunteers to go after the varmints. Now they milled in the street, calling out indignantly, determined to bring the villains to justice.

The sheriff, a tall, stringy man who looked enough like his deputy to be his brother, finally led them off in a cloud of choking dust, which took a long time to settle. Jo watched the departure with mixed feelings. If Slade *did* come, would the few men left in town be up to the job of capturing him and his gang?

None of the remaining men were in evidence. Doc and the supposedly wounded deputy stayed out of sight in Doc's office. The judge had let it be known that he had a sick horse to attend at home, which was why he was leaving Jo in charge of the Mercantile. She thought he had made his way around to the rear of the store and was in the back room now, but she couldn't be sure. She was afraid to go out there and see, because she thought she might be terrified to learn that she was actually there alone, waiting for Slade. The assurances that some of the best shots in the county were placed so as to keep the bandits from reaching her helped scarcely at all.

Nervously, with no customer to wait on, Jo got out her sketch pad and began to draw. It started out to be aimless work with her pencil, but after a time she realized that she had drawn a portrait of Rufus, complete with bruises, split lip, and abraded chin.

She stared at it, swallowed, and closed the pad, putting it away.

It was impossible not to think about Rufus. It wasn't fair, what had happened to him. Not that she'd ever had any reason to think that life was fair. Everybody had bad luck, everybody had accidents, everybody eventually died. She tried to follow Grandma's attitude of making the best of things, but sometimes it was hard.

What could she do to help Rufus, outside of feeding him? She couldn't even do that for long, not without getting caught. And it was the judge's food, so she supposed in a way she was stealing it. Though she thought she was justified, under the circumstances, she wasn't at all sure her uncle would think the same way.

The day dragged on. Every time the door opened she jumped, praying it wouldn't be Slade. That was probably wrong too; she should be hoping he would come in and attempt to steal the nugget from the safe, and be caught. She wanted him caught, all right, but she hated the idea of being there when it happened.

At least she didn't have to worry about Andrew. The judge had arranged for Andrew to spend the day with the Doane boys. They lived over the mortuary, and they were going to help Mr. Doane lay out a body and prepare for a funeral. The idea of it gave Jo the creeps, and she thought Andrew was a little queasy too, though he was curious, as always. He'd seen both Mama and Grandma laid out in the front room before they were buried, so it wasn't as if it would be a totally new experience.

She didn't want to think about dead bodies. If Slade and his gang were captured . . .

"No," she said aloud, then glanced guiltily toward the door to the back room. Had anyone heard her talking to herself? Or was she, in fact, the only one in the building?

She jumped when the front door opened. It was only Miss Susan Brown, wearing the new bonnet, which was most becoming. She smiled at Jo and glanced around as if looking for the owner of the Mercantile.

"Good morning, Josephine. Your uncle isn't here?"

"No. He went back to the house. He's got a sick horse."

Disappointment showed plainly on her face. "Oh. I'm sorry to hear that. I thought surely he'd be here . . . I watched the posse leave so I knew he wasn't with *them*."

"No," Jo said, wishing she knew for certain. "Is there anything I can do for you?"

Miss Brown hesitated, and then, even though they were the only ones in the big room, leaned forward and whispered, "Is it true? Is there an eighty-pound gold nugget in the safe here?"

By tonight, Jo thought wryly, the nugget would be well over one hundred pounds. But, of course, she had to pretend she didn't know anything about anything. "What nugget? Where did you hear such an outrageous thing?"

"You mean there isn't one, after all?"

"I don't know anything about an eighty-pound nugget," Jo said, with complete truthfulness.

"Oh. Well, no doubt they wouldn't want to tell a child—but there's a rumor going around about a valuable nugget that has to be kept in the safe here until old Bill can take the stage out again."

"He's going back on the stage on Monday, I think," Jo said. "His shoulder wasn't broken, you know. He only lost a lot of blood. But I don't know anything about a big nugget." This time she was lying, and she hoped it didn't show.

"Oh. Well, I'm glad he's better. I understand Deputy Shaker was shot this morning, and by the same bandits who held up the stage."

Jo's lips felt stiff, mouthing the lie. "Yes. A posse went out after them."

"Let's hope they get them. My, it's hot, isn't it?" Miss

Brown fanned herself with a limp glove. "I believe I'll go home and take off a few of these petticoats. Maybe," she said, with a wicked little grin, "even walk around barefooted."

"At home," Jo said wistfully, "we went down to the creek and waded in, clothes and all, when it got this hot." Then she wondered if Miss Brown would consider that terribly ill bred.

Miss Brown only sighed. "I'd be tempted to do that myself if there were any stream to do it in except that muddy little trickle. I'd best go on home, I expect. I will see you in church in the morning, won't I?"

If they were all still alive in the morning, Jo thought, but didn't say it. "Yes, of course."

Miss Brown and her questions made Jo nervous, but she was even more uneasy when the lady had gone. There weren't nearly enough customers through the day to occupy either her time or her mind, to keep her from thinking about Slade and worrying about Rufus.

During one lull, while Jo thought longingly of taking off some of her own undergarments and imagined herself back home in the coolness of the Piney Woods, something crashed in the back room.

Immediately her heart burst into a wild tattoo as she swung about, staring at the doorway.

A moment later the judge poked his head out. "It's only me. Knocked over a lantern. Wasn't lit, luckily." He stared beyond her. "No sign of Slade yet, eh?"

Jo massaged her chest with her fingertips, trying to ease the tumult there. "I don't think he'll come into town," she asserted.

The look he gave her was disdainful. "And you're an expert on how the criminal mind works, are you?"

She felt the heat climb into her face, yet held her ground.

"No. But I think he'd be stupid to come. And I don't think he's that stupid. Nasty, but not stupid."

He made a grunting sound. "Well, I hope you're wrong. It's time to stop him."

Having no disagreement with that, Jo remained silent.

Without further comment, the judge turned and went back into the storeroom, closing the door almost all the way.

Jo supposed she ought to have felt better, knowing now for sure that she wasn't alone. But she didn't.

She waited. And waited. And waited.

Slade didn't come, and there was no fusillade of shots from the hidden sharpshooters.

Eventually it was time to lock up and go home, and Jo felt as exhausted as if she'd been running all day, as limp as a wet string.

"What'll happen to the nugget now?" she asked as the judge, looking decidedly grumpy, picked up the cashbox to put it away.

"It'll go on the next stage going east," he said. "Just the way it would have anyway. In the meantime we'll post guards, front and back."

"It'll go on Monday?"

"If old Bill's up to it by then. For somebody who leaked as much blood as he did, his color's pretty good today, so he'll probably go Monday."

They didn't speak again all the way home. They picked up Andrew at the mortuary, and he made up for their silence, chattering about Mrs. Doane's dried-apple pie and how the Doane boys were going to be morticians like their father. "An undertaker can always make a living, even in a little town like Muddy Wells," Andrew said. "Sooner or later everybody needs his services."

Jo didn't want to discuss funerals, and the judge was clearly disgruntled. He had been sure Slade would rise to the bait of a gigantic gold nugget, and he didn't like to be proved wrong.

The first thing Jo did when they entered the kitchen was to check the corn bread—half of it was gone. Rufus had either eaten it plain or remembered to put the butter back down the well.

And she had to do something about supper. Not even the kind of day they'd had could kill their appetites. The house felt like an oven, and she stared disconsolately at the stove.

"What would you eat if we weren't here?" she asked lamely.

The judge finished drinking a dipperful of water before he replied. "Cold corn bread, cold beans, cold potatoes. Is there any of that pie of Mrs. Bacon's left?"

So they ate that, and while it was not particularly satisfying to the taste buds, it at least filled empty stomachs. It didn't set well on Jo's, though; she was too nervous, thinking about Rufus out in the barn, probably hungry again too. Or had he already moved on?

She washed up their few dishes—the water had been standing in the bucket all day, so it was tepid—and at last was able to step out into the backyard.

Around in front of the house she heard Andrew's laughter and the dogs' barking as he played with them. She had left the judge reading a copy of the *Muddy Wells Gazette*, a glum expression on his face. No doubt he had hoped, when next week's edition came out, to read about how Slade's gang had been captured, tried, and sentenced by the Honorable Judge Matthew Macklin.

At any rate, he wasn't paying any attention to her. The remains of corn bread, wrapped in a towel, and a saucer holding the last piece of blackberry pie were concealed in her apron, though if anyone intercepted her he would certainly be able to tell that she was hiding something.

The air was cooling a little now that the sun was low in the western sky, and she walked briskly. There were no horses missing from the pasture as far as she could tell, and she entered the barn with both anticipation and apprehension.

"Rufus?" she called softly. "Are you here?"

There was no immediate response, and disappointment swept over her. He was gone, then. Jo hesitated, biting her lip.

Then there was a stirring sound from the loose hay in the mound opposite the stalls.

"I guess I fell asleep," Rufus said sheepishly, crawling out with bits of hay clinging to his clothes and hair.

Jo was unprepared for the wave of pleasure that surged through her. "I thought you'd gone," she said.

"I would have, except there were too many people around. I figured I'd leave tonight, soon as it gets dark."

"People around? Who?" Jo handed him the food, watching him sink to the floor to eat it. "I forgot a fork, you'll have to eat the pie without one. Who were the people?"

"Well, the judge came back once, but he didn't stay long. Then a lady came and knocked on the door, but when nobody answered, she went away too. And then," Rufus said with his mouth full, "I think I saw Cleet."

"Who's Cleet?" Jo wanted to know. Grandma always said it was a treat to watch a hungry man eat; she sure would have enjoyed watching Rufus dig into the vittles.

"Slade's brother," Rufus said, and Jo stopped breathing for a few seconds.

"What was he doing here?"

"Don't know. Doesn't seem as if I could have left enough

of a trail for him to follow, dry as it is. Umm. You bake this pie?"

"No. Mrs. Bacon did. She comes in once a week. Do you think he saw you?"

"No. If he had, he'd have come after me. He might have been looking for you."

Jo rubbed her arms as if they were cold, though it was still warm enough so she felt sticky. Her voice squeaked when she echoed, "Me?"

Rufus shot her a glance, then devoted himself to finishing off the pie. "Yeah. Slade didn't realize who you were in the store the other day. But he found out the girl who was on the stage was related to that judge, and by listening to the local people talk could have realized the judge owned the Mercantile and where you both lived. So he could have sent Cleet."

Jo's legs were rubbery. "Why would he want me?" she asked, but she already remembered. The sheriff had posted the pictures she had drawn of Slade and Rufus, and since he'd been masked at the time of the stage robbery, he'd know she could only have seen him at the Mercantile. She felt as if someone had punched her in the middle. "You don't think he'd . . . he'd . . ."

"Slade could do anything," Rufus assured her. "That's another reason I hung around until you came home, besides my needing the dark to get away. I wanted to warn you. Tell your uncle so he can make sure you're protected, because Slade doesn't need any more excuse than that he doesn't like you to hurt you. And his brother's often the one who gets to do that part."

Jo stared at him, watching him finish the meal she'd brought, feeling half sick. How could she tell the judge this without telling him where she'd gotten the information?

"And you're sure this Cleet was watching this place?"

"Pretty sure. He didn't come in close, he was down there along the creek, but I've seen him skulking around before, and he's got a hat with a feather in it. Never saw another one like it, and I think I could make that out."

A feather in the band of his hat. "An eagle feather," Jo said slowly as the image formed in her mind. "And he rode a bay mare."

"That's right. You got a good memory," Rufus said. And then, before she could accept the compliment, he added, "Old Slade won't want anyone with a good memory—or the ability to draw pictures that practically bring him to life—to be around to testify against him if they catch him."

"He must know they *will* catch him, sooner or later," Jo said.

"He's been robbing stages and trains and banks for a long time, I think," Rufus told her soberly. "All over Texas. I don't think he ever stayed in one place very long, not long enough to get caught, anyway, until he married Ma and sold off the land. If he'd been around so she'd known what kind of man he was, she'd never have married him, but he can act like a gentleman if he wants to."

Jo was remembering the man's face and she shuddered. She had seen nothing of the gentleman there, only the cruelty, the brutality.

Rufus heaved himself to his feet and handed her the empty saucer. "That was mighty welcome, ma'am. I thank you. I won't bother you anymore. Soon as it's good and dark, I'll be on my way. I want to get as far as I can out of Muddy Wells before daylight, so I may sleep another hour or so."

He was smiling a little, ruefully. "You did such a good job with those pictures of us that they stuck up, I'll have to go some to get where nobody's seen 'em. Reckon anybody would recognize me from that."

Jo swallowed. "I didn't know you weren't . . . a regular member of the gang. I thought you wanted to be a robber."

Rufus grimaced. "I'm afraid everybody's going to think that, so I can't afford to get caught."

"It's your hair that's the most distinctive," Jo told him. "And I'm afraid I told them about it. If you didn't have such bright hair, people would be less likely to notice you."

"I'll keep my hat anchored." He hesitated. "I don't even know your name."

"Josephine. They call me Jo. My whole name's Josephine Eleanor Elizabeth Whitman."

"Jo. I'll remember that. Thanks, Jo, for the supper. And for breakfast this morning too."

She ought to return to the house, she knew, before the judge wondered what she was doing out in the barn, but she was reluctant to bid him good-bye. "You'll need something more to take with you. If you stop and steal anything, you'll have people after you."

"I don't guess a man could starve to death from lack of food for just a few days," Rufus said. "And once I get where there's none of those posters with my picture on 'em, I ought to be able to work for a meal to two."

"Well . . . let me see if I can find anything," Jo offered. "If I do, I'll be back. And if I don't see you again . . . good luck."

She felt exposed, vulnerable, walking back to the house, though it was still daylight enough to see that nobody was lurking under the trees near the shallow creek. Still, the idea of this Cleet, or any of Slade's gang, watching the house was very frightening.

She almost ran up the steps and was gasping for breath when she opened the screen door and entered the house.

The judge had gone into his bedroom and left the door open; the lamplight (for it was dusky inside the house) streamed out across the hallway. She heard him curse and guessed he was working on totaling up sums again, but she didn't offer to help this time.

Instead, she rummaged through the pantry for what she could find that a fleeing man, on foot, could carry. There wasn't a lot—she'd have to have a fire in the stove and cook tomorrow, she thought—but she filled a towel with raw carrots and turnips and some crackers she found in a tin. There was a jar of strawberry jam—probably donated by Mrs. Bacon—and recklessly she put that in too. It was possible her uncle didn't even realize it was there.

The sun had dropped below the horizon now and it was full dusk when she hurried once more through the opening at the end of the barn. Rufus popped up at once.

"Here," she said, thrusting the bundle at him. "It's the best I could do. Good luck, Rufus."

"Thanks, Miss Jo," Rufus said, and Jo felt near tears as she sped back to the house, hearing his words float after her.

She wondered if she'd ever see him again, and she prayed that no one would recognize him and turn him in, even as she cursed herself for drawing his picture in the first place.

If Rufus were caught and tried, it would be her fault, she realized. No one else would have been able to describe him, let alone provide his portrait so anyone would recognize him.

Jo felt thoroughly miserable, and still afraid, as she carried water upstairs to wash in, and got ready for bed and another hot, restless night.

12

Twice during the long, airless night Jo woke to hear the dogs barking.

The second time she rose and went to the window. It was pitch dark; she could see nothing, and the only sounds were of the hounds, out by the barn.

They hadn't barked at Rufus. He had come prepared with tidbits of rabbit meat, and bribed them, and the foolish creatures had licked the juice off his fingers and wagged their tails.

Was there someone out there, or were the dogs barking at nothing, the way dogs sometimes do?

She thought of the man called Cleet, brother of Tom Slade, who had been lurking along the creek yesterday. Why had he come? Did it have to do with the judge—perhaps to steal horses from him—or with herself? Or could he, in spite of what Rufus believed, have followed the youngest bandit here? Was he out there now?

Below, on the porch, the screen door slammed and the judge's shrill whistle cut through the heavy air, followed by a profane shout to the dogs to cease their racket.

For a few seconds the barking stopped, then one of the dogs gave a few halfhearted yips and fell silent.

The air was so sultry it was hard to breathe. Jo stood for a few minutes, willing the air to turn cooler, but nothing happened, of course. After a bit she turned and went back to bed, wishing that her uncle had locked the doors, knowing he hadn't. Every door and window stood open to whatever cool breeze might stir. Jo stared up into the blackness, sure she would not sleep again before dawn.

She did, however, waking when the sun was well up, its light flooding her room.

Another hot day, and a Sunday, to boot. She wondered if anyone would notice if she left off a few layers of undergarments, decided they would (Grandma always had), and dressed reluctantly and sluggishly. Mostly she'd always liked being a girl, but on hot days she envied Andrew and the other boys, who didn't have to have all those layers of petticoats and skirts.

The judge was up and had the stove going; she could smell coffee and bacon. She knew the heat was going to be a blow when she walked into the kitchen, causing her to wince, but as long as there was a fire she might as well make up a supply of corn bread, and there was enough of the white flour left for another batch of biscuits. While she was at it, she decided to cook potatoes and boil some of the eggs to make potato salad later.

"Can't imagine what was wrong with those fool hounds last night," the judge grumbled when they sat down to eat. "I suppose the weather's making everybody jumpy, even the dogs."

Jo wanted to tell him that one or more of the bandits might have been out there, but she couldn't. Not without revealing that she'd talked to Rufus, and sending another posse after him.

"Better gather the eggs and put them in a basket, down the well. They won't keep long in temperatures like this," the judge said.

So Jo went out into the barnyard, and fed the chickens, and fended off old Rusty, and then, pretending unconcern, stepped into the barn.

The smell of manure and alfalfa was strong, but that was all that was there. Rufus was gone. Jo hoped he had traveled a long way last night.

The hounds roused lazily to wag their tails at her, halfway between the house and the barn. Jo greeted them soberly. "I wish you were more reliable," she told them, and allowed them to lick the hand that wasn't carrying the egg basket.

The judge had brought out the ledgers again and was muttering under his breath as he added up the figures. Jo eyed his stubbly face and asked tentatively, "You're going to shave before we go to church, aren't you?"

He looked up, startled, scowling. "Church?"

"You promised Miss Brown you'd take us to services."

The scowl deepened. "I suppose that's what Ma would do, eh?"

"Grandma never missed Sabbath services. And you said we'd go."

The judge shoved back his chair with exasperation. "It'll be hot enough in that church to barbecue a pig," he predicted, but he was moving. Maybe Grandma had planted some of the right standards in him after all.

After she'd finished up in the kitchen, and the fire was being allowed to die out, Jo took a sponge bath before she dressed for church. She chose her best dress, and then went over to Andrew's room to slick down his hair with water and make sure he'd washed behind his ears. Grandma used to say that left to his own devices, he'd have had enough dirt back there to plant peas.

Sunday services were both a time of worship and an opportunity for sociability in Muddy Wells, the same as they were at home. People dressed in their best met in the churchyard to visit both before and after the preaching and the singing, and the main topic of conversation was the bandits who had robbed the stage and also the bank over at Dry Creek Station. They speculated on whom the bandits would attack next.

Bill, the stage driver, was there, looking his old ruddy self. "Takes more'n a bullet to keep me down for long," he told Jo, grinning. "I'll be ready to roll again by morning. Fact is, I could go right now, but I been invited to a chicken dinner at the Widow Farley's after the services."

Miss Brown was as pretty as a Texas bluebonnet in her blue dress and the new hat with the blue ribbons. She had waved and smiled when they entered the church, and intercepted them on the doorstep when they left.

It was clearly the judge she was interested in, so Jo sidled away to give them some privacy. If Mrs. Bacon was right, and the judge was so difficult to deal with because his sweetheart had run off with another man, perhaps finding a new lady would improve his disposition. Not in time to do Jo and Andrew any good, of course. They'd be returning to the Piney Woods to live with Aunt Harriet before it was likely the courting would be done and a wedding would take place.

Andrew had run on ahead to meet the Doane boys. Jo was glad he'd made friends, and wished she had too. The girl who had introduced herself earlier smiled in her direction but kept on talking with her friends, not approaching Jo.

Her thoughts kept returning to Rufus, wondering how far he'd managed to get on foot, and whether or not any of Slade's men would have tried to follow him. Jo began to walk slowly toward home.

She didn't mean to get quite so far ahead of the others,

though. When she turned onto the street that led to the judge's house, she suddenly became aware that neither Andrew nor the judge was with her. She stopped, abruptly unwilling to go any closer to home by herself.

She could see the house, its white paint reflecting the sunshine, and the cottonwoods behind it, and the barn. Nothing stirred. Not even Rusty and his harem pecked around in the chicken yard. She didn't see the dogs, but friendly old things that they were, they'd provide no protection.

Jo stood at the corner, waiting for the judge to catch up with her. He must like Miss Brown, at least a little bit, to stand talking with her this long.

Gradually something odd about the placid scene before her nudged into her consciousness. Jo stiffened, feeling a rush of perspiration break out, which dried so quickly in the heat that she felt immediately chilled.

Jo edged along the side of the house on the corner, then back out onto Main Street. A quick glance revealed that the judge and Miss Brown were coming this way, would be here in a few minutes. The chill had gone, the perspiration remained, and she stood there until they reached her.

"My goodness," Miss Brown said, quickening her last few steps. "You're white as a cotton boll. Have you had your bonnet off? You aren't getting sunstroke, are you, child?"

Jo moistened her lips. "No, ma'am, I don't believe so. I'm used to heat, and I didn't bare my head. But I think—" She looked at her uncle and swallowed, reluctant to say the words. "I can't see any horses," she said.

"Horses?" Miss Brown echoed, mystified.

The judge was quicker to understand. He stared toward his own barn and corrals and let out a muffled exclamation. "If that boy forgot to close the gate—"

He left the implied threat unspoken, but broke into a trot, leaving the two females standing there to follow at a slower pace.

"Oh, dear. I hope poor Andrew isn't in trouble—"

"Andrew wouldn't leave a gate open," Jo stated positively. "He was born on a farm. He knows about gates and livestock."

Miss Brown was uncertain. "But what else—"

Jo's voice had a tremor in it. "There is a gang of men loose," she said, recalling the barking dogs late last night, "who think nothing of holding up banks and stages and shooting people. If they needed horses—"

And there had been Cleet, skulking along in the cover of the cottonwoods, perhaps seeking neither Rufus nor Jo but valuable horses, yet she couldn't say anything about that.

Alarm washed over Miss Brown's face. "*Those* men . . . oh, dear! Matthew!"

The last was called out, and the judge, who had not gotten so very far ahead of them, paused, looking over his shoulder. "There had better not be any of those varmints on my place," he said. "Surely they wouldn't dare come after my horses. . . ."

Miss Brown twisted her gloves. "Matthew, you're not armed. Wouldn't it be a good idea to call the sheriff to go with you?"

He gave her one of those looks men reserve for women who are being absurd and kept on going, leaving the two females to trail along in his dust.

She'd called the judge *Matthew*. If Jo hadn't been so concerned, she'd have been pleased. Grandma had often observed that many a man only became a *good* man because he found a good woman who stood with him through thick and thin and kept him from doing anything foolish.

She wasn't sure anyone could stop the judge from doing

whatever he chose, foolish or not. However, she had no hesitation in following close behind him. He might not be armed, but he was a force to be reckoned with, and she didn't think Cleet or anyone else from the Slade gang would want to confront him. Not when a single shot from a six-shooter would bring the whole town within minutes. Besides, she had the uneasy conviction that the horses were long gone, and the bandits with them.

The judge's rigid stance and angrily reddening face, the open gate, told Jo she was right before she and Miss Brown ever reached the barn. There was not a horse in either the corral or the pasture. Even the judge's favorite riding horse was not to be seen.

The judge's fury was monumental. If he'd had the thieves there at the moment, it seemed likely they would never have been allowed to come to trial.

"Oh, Matthew! All of them?" Miss Brown whispered.

"The dogs barked—" Jo began, but her uncle cut her off with a contemptuous glance.

"The dogs barked, late at night. You think I should have taken a gun and gone out to investigate?" he practically snarled. Grandma said men often become furiously angry with everyone else when they themselves are even partially responsible for whatever mess they're in. "Those fool hounds bark at their own shadows. If I went out every time they bark, I'd never get any sleep at all."

It seemed to Jo that one reason for having dogs was to give warning that something was amiss, and if one didn't investigate when they barked—or became accustomed to allowing them to yap at nothing—one could scarcely blame the dogs. She doubted that even Grandma would have been brave enough to say as much to the judge at this moment, however.

"The horses were all here when we left for church," the judge stated, as if expecting someone to challenge that. "I saw them. And when I get them back, I guarantee the thieves a speedy trial and execution."

He spun on his heel and started toward the house. Jo wouldn't have been surprised if there had been smoke coming out both his ears.

Miss Brown sighed in distress. "Men put such store in their horses," she mused. "I was so hoping that this would prove to be a special day, and now it's all spoiled. But of course that's of small importance. Something dreadful has taken place, and he blames himself—"

"The dogs *did* bark during the night. He swore at them and told them to shut up."

Her smile was wry. "Yes. And now I suppose he's going to set off for help to track them down. So much for our pleasant Sunday afternoon."

So much for my own peace of mind too, Jo thought as they walked toward the house where the judge had vanished inside.

What if it hadn't been Cleet at all who had driven off the horses? What if Rufus had decided that he had little chance of getting out of the county on foot, leaving him with no choice, as he might have seen it, except to steal one from the judge.

He could easily have waited until the family had left for church, knowing they'd be gone plenty long enough for him to act. He might have chosen one horse and led it off, taking no care with the remaining stock by closing the gate, and in time they'd all wandered off.

No, she tried to tell herself, he wouldn't have done that. Even if he'd felt compelled to "borrow" a horse, feeling desperate to get away and convinced it would be impossible without a mount, Rufus was a farm boy. He knew the importance of closing gates. He would have done it without thinking, simply because he'd been brought up that way, the same as she had.

Not Rufus. Cleet, or Slade, or the whole band was far more likely.

It didn't make her feel any better, though. She could only speculate about everything, and fear of what was going to happen now stuck fast in her throat.

She walked into the house, holding the door for Miss Brown, to meet the judge in the kitchen. He was fastening on his gun belt, and his mouth was grim.

13

Miss Brown stayed on after the judge had gone, to keep the children company, she said. Jo suspected it was as much for her own sake as for Jo's and Andrew's; she wanted to be there when the judge came home.

She helped make the potato salad and fry a couple of chickens; they had agreed that they would cook the chicken before it got any hotter. Miss Brown didn't attempt to take charge of the kitchen, as many adults would have done. She asked what she could do to help, offered specifics such as setting the table, and in general behaved as if the decisions were Jo's to make. It was obvious that she'd never been in the judge's house before. Though she didn't comment on anything, Jo couldn't miss seeing that Miss Brown noticed everything from the antimacassars on the green overstuffed furniture in the unused parlor to the brass bed visible through the open doorway into the judge's bedroom. Her eyes were bright with interest in everything.

Jo had mixed feelings about the lady being there. On one hand, she wanted to be free of other distractions, so she could think about Rufus and worry about him without being questioned in regard to her moodiness. On the other, she would have been uneasy, alone in the house with Andrew for any period of time. It was too isolated, here on the edge of town, and it was clear that Slade and his gang members knew where the judge lived, and therefore where she was, as well.

She thought they had taken a terrible risk, coming here to steal the judge's horses in broad daylight, even if it was at a time when virtually the entire town was singing hymns and listening to the preaching. The bandits had perfectly good horses, so they hadn't acted out of desperation on that score. It seemed to Jo that it was more an act of bravado, of challenge, a sort of "catch us if you can" attitude designed to infuriate not only the judge but the entire population of Muddy Wells.

Well, it had certainly succeeded insofar as the judge was concerned.

It hadn't taken long to round up a posse this time. The men had inspected the corral, the gate, the pasture behind the barn, the area along the nearly dry creek bed, and then had galloped off to the south. Eventually the dust they had stirred up drifted to the veranda and settled on the trio watching from there.

"I wish they'd let me go with a posse," Andrew said wistfully.

Jo gave silent thanks that they hadn't.

After that, there was nothing to do but wait. And wait. And wait.

It was dusk before the men returned. Judge Macklin was no less dour than when he had departed. He washed his face and hands and slumped in a kitchen chair while Jo silently brought out the food.

"I had to borrow a horse to go after them," he said, his

fury tempered only a little by his fatigue. "And we only brought back two horses, out of a dozen. Not Jury," he added, glancing at Andrew.

"But you did pick up their trail, then," Miss Brown said, sipping at the lemonade that wasn't cold enough to be really refreshing.

"Oh, yes, we did that. As near as we could tell, it was only one man ran them off. At least we only found one set of boot prints."

Jo's heart sank. Not the entire gang. But not Rufus, either, she prayed.

"We found two stragglers that got separated from the others. The rest were driven over the rocks. We couldn't pick up the trail again. And there's another thing."

Jo waited, her mouth dry.

"There's been someone in my barn. Overnight, at least, from the look of it."

Jo only just resisted the urge to press a palm against her chest over the tumult there. She suspected she'd gone pale, but hoped that would be attributed to the heat, or perhaps would not be noticed at all in the lamplight.

Miss Brown's face revealed her concern. "You think he was there this morning? Waiting for you to leave for church so he could steal the horses?"

"I'd bet on it," the judge said harshly. "And when we catch up with him, he'll find out what happens to people who steal horses in my county."

Jo found it difficult to breathe. When she had put the chicken and potato salad on the table for him, she decided it might be best to leave him alone with Miss Brown. *She* might be able to calm him down.

Jo pushed Andrew ahead of her, out the back door and

into the yard. The boy was excited about the whole thing. "I'd like to be there when they catch the thief. Do you suppose they'll hang him on the spot? I mean, what's the use of a trial when they'll know he's guilty if they catch him with any of the horses, won't they?"

Jo swallowed and tried to sound normal. "The law says everybody's entitled to a trial."

In the fading light Andrew's face showed disappointment. "I suppose that's right. Well, I'd still like to be there when they catch him."

The sky was a pale blue edged with pink along the horizon, deepening in a darker hue overhead. Jo could even see the first stars appearing in its depths. It was a time she had always loved, when the heat of the day began to fade and the breath of night sweetened the air.

But she couldn't enjoy it tonight. If they caught Rufus—whether or not he had driven off the horses, he would still be accused of being a member of Slade's gang—there would be a trial. The result was a foregone conclusion. Her own drawing would help to convict him.

She could only hope that Rufus had traveled many miles since she'd seen him, that he was far beyond the reach of the Muddy Wells authorities. That he would find an honest job and never come back here.

Yet a part of her grieved that she would never know what had become of the young fugitive who had never wanted to be a bandit in the first place.

She stayed outside, walking around the yard, listening to Andrew playing some exciting game with imaginary companions, until it was full dark. Only then did she return, reluctantly, to the house.

* * *

The sky had a brassy, threatening appearance as they walked along Main Street the following morning. "Rain?" Jo asked uncertainly, looking up at it.

"Or worse. Wind, maybe tornadoes." The judge was surlier than ever this morning. He had eaten in silence after announcing that Jo would have to be at the Mercantile again today.

"I'll be on the stage when it leaves—" He paused for a moment to curse the fate that had left him without horses. "I have to go over to Dry Gulch for a trial. Horse thief and murderer. I'll stay for the hanging, then be home by the end of the week."

Andrew had, as usual, run on ahead, pursuing a tumbleweed that he pretended was a bandit that he must capture. Jo's mind wasn't on her brother, however, but on the prospect of being alone in the house while Slade's gang was still on the loose. True, they'd be at the Mercantile during the day and Miss Brown had agreed to stay with them at night, but Jo doubted Miss Brown would be of much use against Slade if he showed up.

As they passed the Grand Hotel—which was in Jo's opinion about as ungrand as a hotel could be—they saw that the stage was being loaded for its run to the east. Old Bill wasn't lifting any boxes and trunks to the roof. He had a pair of adolescent boys doing that work, though he no longer wore a sling.

He greeted them cheerfully. "Morning, Judge! Missy! Looks like we might be in for a bit of weather, eh, before the day's over? Settle the dust if there's rain in it."

The judge critically assessed the way the baggage had been arranged. "Half that load's going to fall off the back if you have to put the team to a run."

Bill turned, cursed, and spat tobacco juice into the street. "Here, you, take that down and start over again! It won't stay that way!" He gave them explicit and profane instructions on how to do it right, then spoke again to the judge. "Be over to the Mercantile as soon as we're ready and the passengers show up. Two of 'em spent the evening at the Silver Dollar and they're not feeling too well this morning." He smiled broadly, as if this amused him. "Looks to be more onlookers than usual today. Shouldn't wonder if they're not curious about the cargo I'll be picking up over to the Mercantile." Bill gave a conspiratorial wink in Jo's direction.

"Well, don't say anything to anyone to suggest that you're picking up anything of importance," the judge growled, touching Jo's arm. "Let's get over there. Oh." He paused to look back at the stage driver. "You've got someone riding shotgun, haven't you?"

"Oh, sure. Tommy Duelle up on top and"—he gave another wink—"two more armed men inside as passengers. Not the ones who drank too much last night, but dead shots, both of 'em." He spat into the dust at his feet. "Hear the ruckus this morning, did you?"

Immediately Judge Macklin's expression turned wary. "What ruckus was that?"

Bill chuckled. "Took just about everybody who was around and about that time of morning to straighten it out."

The wariness became alarm, and the judge looked across the street toward the Mercantile. "Not *everybody*, I hope," he said, and Bill was quick to reassure him.

"No, no, not *them*, Yer Honor. See, there's Wister in plain sight of the front door." Wister, Jo knew, was the man who had taken this shift guarding the safe. "Didn't none of your men desert their posts. They're all too smart to be taken in by a con-trived di-version, and this weren't a fire or shooting or anything that would have made even them come running."

The judge didn't look totally convinced. "Lower your voice, you fool. Or at least watch your words." His own voice dropped. "Our *expected visitors* wouldn't shoot off guns or set a fire for a diversion if they could think of anything else. Either one would bring the whole town on the run, and it's unlikely they'd want that. What was the commotion then?"

"Oh, them steers old Babcock brung in off the range yesterday. Put 'em in that corral behind his barn—he's fixing to trade steers for some of Harrington's horses—and somebody was careless with a gate. Confounded critters got to churning around, knocked the gate open, and danged if the whole batch of 'em didn't come right on through town, spooked so they was on a regular rampage. Had us a proper rodeo, we did. Too bad you missed it."

"Spooked by what?" the judge asked with heavy suspicion, still looking at the guard posted opposite the Mercantile, as if carelessly lounging there picking his teeth.

"Aw, who knows what it takes to spook a herd of steers? Anyway, they was running and slamming into each other and everything in their path. Miz Purcell nearly got trampled and jumped into the doorway at the Silver Dollar, and one of them critters actually went through the window at the Cozy Corner right at breakfast time. Everybody in there, and everyone 'twas around opening up their businesses, come out and helped round 'em up and head 'em back to Babcock's corral. All settled down within twenty minutes, no harm done except to the window at the Cozy Corner. I wouldn'ta been surprised if you'd heard the yelling and swearing all the way over to your place, Judge."

Jo could tell by her uncle's face that even though old Bill

thought it was a lark, the judge wasn't totally convinced the episode hadn't been something contrived by Slade's gang.

The judge grunted and hurried Jo with him, on along the street, their heels thudding on the boardwalk. Wister saw them coming and lifted a hand in a lazy salute to indicate that everything was all right.

Jo cleared her throat. It was undoubtedly safer to remain silent, but she had always found that to be difficult. "Do you think Slade and his gang will try to ambush the stage?"

"I'll be surprised if they don't. It pays to be prepared. Slade may have reconnoitered enough to figure out we had men posted all through town and figured it would be easier to take on just a coachful, rather than the entire town, but we're not making it easy for him. I'll be on the stage too and I also am armed. The gang won't surprise us or outnumber us with guns this time." The way he said it was chilling.

Wister walked to meet them as they reached the steps of the Mercantile, and the judge paused to speak to him as Jo accepted the key and opened the front door. She heard the guard say, "Oh, I had to jump out of the way, but I didn't leave my post, Your Honor. Kept an eye on that front door every minute."

"Who's out back?" the judge asked as Jo turned the key. "Salicky, isn't it?"

A burst of stale air greeted her when she entered the store, intermingling the smells of dried fruit and cheese and leather boots and licorice.

Jo wrinkled her nose. The place had been closed up tight since Saturday evening, and the odors that would have been all right individually formed a composite that was distinctively unpleasant.

She wondered if it would be all right to leave the front door open to air the place out. Perhaps if the back door was open too, that might do the job more quickly.

Jo took off her bonnet and put it on a low shelf behind the counter, then walked through into the back room.

Her feet suddenly took root in the wooden floor. For a moment she could scarcely credit the sight that met her eyes.

Her jaw dropped and her mouth went so dry that when she tried to speak her first effort was no more than a squeak. "Oh, no! Oh, dear . . ."

The first thing she became aware of was that the back door into the storeroom had been pried open and hung in splinters from a single hinge.

That was hardly the worst of it. The big iron safe, the one that held the cashbox and the ledgers and had for several days given space to the great golden nugget, had also been opened.

The door stood ajar, and except for the ledgers, the safe was empty.

Jo made a futile sound of distress, and the judge stepped to the doorway behind her.

"What's the matter?"

Before he'd finished the words, however, his own eyes swept the scene. Jo watched his countenance take on a crimson hue, which rapidly faded away to a sickly pallor beneath his tan.

Grandma's reaction to adversity had always been to pray. It wasn't praying that Judge Macklin did now, however. Jo knew she ought to cover her ears against the language he was using, but she hadn't the strength to lift her hands that far.

He brushed past her, kicking aside the remains of the door to the alley, and peered out. For a moment he too had trouble with speech, and then he spoke to Jo without looking at her. "Go see if Wister is still there. If he isn't, run fetch Doc Scobie yourself."

He was already gone, out into the alley, and Jo paused long enough to look after him, her heart pounding wildly when she saw the crumpled figure outside the back door. The man called Salicky had been with the posse yesterday. She recognized his plaid shirt, though at that time it hadn't been soaked in blood from a vicious head wound.

Jo swallowed and bolted back through the store to relay the order.

Wister blanched but departed on his errand without questions, and Jo returned to the scene of the disaster, dreading to learn the extent of it.

Her uncle was kneeling beside the unfortunate Salicky and looked up when she spoke.

"Is he . . . dead?"

"Not yet." The judge stood up, his words grim. "Well, you were right about one thing. Slade was smarter than we were." There was little satisfaction in his admission, either for Jo or for himself. "It wasn't likely old Babcock's hired man would have failed to secure a gate, and as far as I'm concerned this proves it. Slade sent those steers through the street to make a racket and hold people's attention long enough for him to break in my back door. If Salicky cried out while it was going on, nobody heard him, or the smashing of the door. He probably turned toward the racket, wondering about it even if he didn't go investigate, and that made it easier for someone to walk up behind him and hit him over the head." He swore again, and Jo thought probably even Grandma might have forgiven him, under the circumstances.

"Not much doubt about who's guilty here," he said finally, when he could speak without choking on his rage. "Recognize that horse, do you?"

Bewildered, Jo went out onto the doorstep and followed his gaze. Beyond the alley there were only the backyards, mostly hidden behind high wooden fences, of the houses on the next street. At the bottom of the steps in the adjoining building, however, stood a horse, reins looped over a post.

It was a small, sturdy, ugly animal that Jo would never be able to forget.

Rufus called the paint Comanche. Even while Jo fought against believing the evidence as the judge saw it, she knew what everyone would think: that Rufus had been one of those who had stolen the cashbox and the nugget, though it didn't make sense that he'd have left the horse behind at the scene of the crime.

She stood there, numbed, as the judge brushed by her, now in a silence even more menacing than his words had been, to meet the men whose feet sounded out front.

It wasn't Rufus, Jo thought desperately. The horse had thrown him and run off; otherwise the boy wouldn't have been hiding in the barn but would have been out of the county before the rest of the gang could find him.

Hardly daring to think what would happen now if they caught Rufus, she felt an overwhelming urge to cry, but she had never been the weepy sort. She wouldn't start now.

She was like Grandma, her uncle had said. Yet she hadn't a clue as to what Grandma would have done in a situation like this. She couldn't even summon what it took to pray.

She leaned against the splintered door frame, shaking, and waited.

14

Jo watched and listened to them, the sheriff, the deputy, the judge, and several other important men in the town who were included in the discussion of what the authorities would do to track down the thieves.

"We shouldn't never have kept that confounded nugget in town and leaked the fact that we had it," someone said. Jo didn't know who he was, but he looked important, with a fancy gold watch chain draped across a flowered waistcoat.

The judge glared at him, and Jo withdrew as far from the angry men as she could get, behind the counter. It was past time for the Mercantile to be open for business, but so far the CLOSED sign still hung on the front door, though the door wasn't locked.

The sheriff hooked his thumbs in his belt and spoke in a soft Texas drawl. "Don't recollect that you said so at the time we discussed it, Henry. We thought it had a good chance of working."

"Well, it didn't work, did it?" the man called Henry retorted. "And here we are, responsible for somebody else's gold nugget that got stole because it was in the safe here. What we going to do about it?"

"We're going to get it back," Deputy Shaker said. He was angry too, Jo saw, but he was angry with an icy cold, while the judge was furiously hot. Her uncle looked as if he might explode at any minute.

Henry didn't seem to notice. "And how we going to do that, may I ask? We've had posses chasing those bandits over two counties for weeks, and nobody's so much as got a shot at them so far. Even," he added, making it clear that he was speaking pointedly to the deputy, "when they had a chance."

A nerve jumped in Mr. Shaker's cheek, and his Adam's apple bobbed as he spoke. "If I'd got into a gun battle with five armed men, me with one six-gun and the stage driver already shot, you'd have been the first one to scream if some of the passengers had been killed. You don't sound like you got anything productive to offer, Henry, so why don't you go on back to the Bar Lone Star and let the rest of us handle this?"

Now it was Henry's turn to turn red. "Six of my men rode with those posses every time you called for volunteers. I got a stake in this, the same as everyone else. And everybody knows I got the biggest ranch in the county, the most horses, the most cattle. I got a lot to lose if you don't stop that gang."

"Everybody in Muddy Wells's got a lot to lose if we don't stop them," Sheriff Dalton said. "But we will, Henry. Go home and let us get on with it."

"You think they're going to hang around with that nugget?" Henry wanted to know. "They're probably halfway to Waco by now."

"Then we'll go halfway to Waco to get 'em," the sheriff assured him. "All the way, if need be."

Their record hadn't been that great so far, Jo thought, but she too was relieved when the man called Henry left. She wondered if the others would be in terrible trouble because they'd held the nugget in the judge's safe, though it was true that with their stage driver shot they couldn't have moved it much sooner. And they *had* set guards, two here at the Mercantile and others at strategic places along the street where they were supposedly watching for the gang. They must all have been distracted by the steers running through town though, because it didn't seem they'd noticed Slade and his men when they came.

A fist rapped on the front door and it opened to admit Bill, the stage driver. "Ready to load up that nug—"

He stopped when he saw the assembled men. "Sorry, Judge, thought you was alone."

"It's gone," the judge said grimly. "They broke in my back door during the time Babcock's cattle were stampeding, left a lame horse out in the alley, and got away with the nugget slick as a whistle. One of them's a safecracker, obviously. It couldn't have taken them very long."

Bill's jaw dropped. He trotted over to look into the back room and eventually came back shaking his head. "It's one of their horses, all right. That Slade gang. Belonged to the kid, the one collected the valuables. Wasn't anybody watching this place?"

Deputy Shaker cleared his throat. "Wister, out front, never saw a thing except the stampede. Salicky was in the back. He got hit over the head, knocked out. Doc says he'll probably be all right, but he never even heard anything."

"Well, shoot," Bill said, scratching through his three-day beard. "What I better do, then? Just take off without it?"

"What might be better," the sheriff said thoughtfully, "is to decide you can't drive quite yet, Bill. Need another day or two to recuperate."

"I'm all right," Bill protested, then subsided. "Oh. You

think you can get it back in a day or two? And we wouldn't have to explain to the fellas on the other end that it got away from us?"

The judge's voice was harsh with strain. "I have to be in Dry Gulch tomorrow for a trial."

The sheriff took his thumbs out from behind his belt and straightened up. "That's what they got the telegraph for, Your Honor. Send a wire over to the Gulch and tell them they'll have to postpone the trial a day or two. Probably won't matter to the prisoner if he hangs tomorrow or next week, far as that goes."

"Is there any chance we can recover that nugget in twenty-four hours?" the judge asked, sounding as if he already knew the answer and it wasn't the one he wanted.

"We have some tracks out back, including one horse with a distinctive shoe, and one witness who saw four men riding out of town while the steers were being herded back to their corral. They headed east."

"Which means they could have ridden far enough to get out of sight and then swung back to the south and west," the judge said. "Fat lot of help that is."

"I sent a man out to try to pick up the trail, soon as I heard," Sheriff Dalton said. "Joe Turtle. He's the best tracker I know of. If they swung off the main road, there's a good chance he'll spot where they did it."

"All right. Go get them," the judge said. "I'll send the telegram, say I'm delayed for a day. But that's all. I can't wait any longer than that, even if we have to admit we lost the nugget. I don't trust that bunch over at the Gulch not to string the prisoner up without benefit of trial if we don't get it done legal pretty soon."

Bill was still scratching through his whiskers. "Stage company's going to be pretty mad if we don't turn up with that nugget first trip out."

Nobody disputed that statement, and the men split up. The judge flipped the sign on the front door after they'd gone and gave Jo a sour look. "First thing, I need to replace that back door. Then I'd better take that walleyed paint over home and turn him loose in the pasture where he'll have grass and water." His mouth was grim. "He's not much of a trade for my own good horses. When we get hold of that kid, he'd better be able to tell me what he did with them."

Jo sought desperately for something to say that wouldn't give away her own guilty knowledge. "It doesn't make sense that he—that Rufus—would have left his own horse behind. He knows a lot of people saw it when the stage was robbed, that we know it belongs to him."

"It's lame," the judge told her. "He couldn't ride it out of here in a hurry."

"Then it must have been lame when he brought it in, wasn't it? Why would he do that? He isn't stupid!"

"Anybody who robs a safe in my store is stupid," the judge informed her on his way into the back room, "because he isn't going to get away with it."

"There were other tracks, weren't there? Other horses?"

"Half a dozen, counting the paint."

"But you said the witness only saw four men riding out." Not Rufus, she thought. He hadn't been with them, he hadn't been the one to bring his horse here.

The judge shrugged. "They may not have all left together. But that's the boy's horse, all right."

He began to clean up the mess around the back door, throwing the debris out into the alley where Salicky's blood was still visible in dark stains in the dirt.

Jo's heart fluttered as she struggled to find words to exonerate Rufus, but she couldn't tell her uncle what she knew, that the boy had lost the horse days earlier. It was clear to her that it been left here to implicate him. The judge, however, was convinced that Rufus was guilty along with the rest of the gang, and if he didn't manage to get away . . . Her throat closed, and she couldn't say anything more.

The day blurred in Jo's mind as she went through the motions of waiting on customers. It was made more difficult by the gossiping and curiosity of those customers; they all knew about the stage robbery, if not about the latest disaster with the gold nugget, and scarcely anyone had failed to notice that the sheriff and his deputy were moving around today with what seemed specific purpose.

As the judge's niece, Jo was assumed to have access to more information than the other women, and time after time she was forced to evade their questions or tell outright lies by saying she didn't know what was going on.

And the whole time she was worried sick about Rufus, and what would happen if anyone caught him.

The judge had fixed the back door, then left her in charge at the store. By the end of the day, he hadn't come back, and she heard nothing from or about the law officers. It was time to close up, so Jo locked the doors, checking each of them twice, and let herself out onto the wooden sidewalk. She went past the mortuary, three doors down, to pick up Andrew. He related a rather gruesome story about what he'd learned there that day, and Jo grimaced. "Let's talk about something else," she suggested as they walked toward home.

"It's interesting, Jo," Andrew told her earnestly. "Even making the coffins is sort of interesting. I got to help pound some of the nails today. I like the smell of the wood too. When they're put together, Mr. Doane stacks them in the back room. He only makes a few at a time, because usually there aren't a lot of deaths all at once—"

Jo shivered. "I should hope not. Come on, walk faster. If Uncle Matthew's home he'll be hungry."

The judge wasn't there, however. They ate a cold supper, Jo saying little as Andrew jabbered away with enthusiasm about the funeral business. It had been easier, Jo thought, when he was entranced with the idea of being a deputy sheriff.

"I kind of like it here," he said as Jo began to clear the table. "Except it's so hot and there's no place to swim. Back home I'd be splashing around in the creek right now, cooling off."

Jo felt the same way about it, but the piddling little trickle that passed for a creek here would scarcely allow one to wet one's ankles, and then in tepid water.

She sighed as she dipped water into the dishpan and put in the dishes. How wonderful it would be to take off most of her clothes and wade into a deep, cool stream!

She reached up to unbutton the neck of her dress, fanning herself a little. Nothing helped much.

She had finished the dishes and was debating whether to take her sketch pad outside and draw a picture of the ugly little horse out by the barn, or to sit on the porch with the latest issue of *Godey's Lady's Book*. Only one coveted copy came to Muddy Wells each month; it was usually sold to the banker's wife, and then passed around among the other ladies until it was worn out, Miss Brown had told her. Jo intended to be very careful with it, so that the eventual buyer would not have reason for complaint at its condition.

Before she had decided, though, the judge's footsteps sounded on the back porch. Jo turned to face him, juggling apprehension and anticipation.

Her uncle's expression was not promising. He carried a folded page of what she recognized with a sinking heart as the sketch pad she had used while at the Mercantile. She suddenly remembered what the last drawing had been, and a knot formed in her middle.

He thrust it at her in an almost violent gesture. "When did you draw this?" he demanded.

It seemed as if her heart stopped, and she forgot that only moments ago she had been drenched in perspiration. The chill went all the way through her.

"S-several days ago," she admitted. She could hardly deny the sketch was hers, of Rufus with swollen, scabbed-over lips, and the deep bruise on one cheekbone.

His tone was accusing. "You didn't show him this way in the first sketch I saw."

Not knowing how to reply without giving everything away, Jo remained silent. Her mind raced, but it wasn't going anywhere. No acceptable explanation occurred to her.

He stared into her face, searching it. Then something shifted in his expression, and he reached toward her.

"What's this? The locket? The locket that was stolen when the stage was robbed?"

Her face must have given her away even without any words. The judge's face hardened as he grasped the thin chain and lifted the locket itself out of its resting place beneath her clothes. Why hadn't it occurred to her that when she unbuttoned the dress because of the heat the chain might be exposed?

"How did you get it back?" he asked, and his voice was like the slash of a whip across her flesh.

Jo swallowed hard. "I . . . he brought it back."

"The boy? That Rufus? When did he do this?"

Jo guessed what it must be like to confront this man in the courtroom, knowing the judge had the power of life and death over the accused. She stepped away from him when he let the locket drop back into place, reaching out a hand to the back of a chair to steady herself.

"He's the one who stole my horses, isn't he? You knew it, yet you never said so."

"No," Jo choked. "No, he didn't do that. I know he didn't. He didn't leave his horse behind the Mercantile, either, he wouldn't have been that stupid. Besides"—and now that the words had begun to erupt she couldn't seem to stop them—"he didn't have the horse. It had thrown him and run off; he couldn't catch it."

He didn't believe her. It was clearly written on his countenance. "And without a horse he could ride, he wasn't the one who stole mine?"

Tears blurred her vision. "It's true," she quavered. "Slade and his gang were the ones who stole the horses, and undoubtedly they were the ones who robbed the safe too. That's why there were only four of them leaving town. Rufus wasn't with them. They had beaten him up for returning the locket, and he didn't want to be one of the gang in the first place! Slade was his stepfather, and he made him do those things! That's why Rufus didn't have a gun when they held up the stage, because Slade didn't trust him with one. Remember, I told you Slade hit his hand with a gun when he hesitated about taking my locket. And then Slade beat him up, and Rufus was running away when his horse fell and threw him; that's why he's lame—the horse, I mean—and he kept on running. Rufus, that is. He's not one of the bandits, not really, and—"

Jo broke off, seeing that her words were having no effect. There was too much evidence against her.

"That's enough. Go upstairs and stay in your room until I tell you to come out. The boy was in my barn, wasn't he? You even fed him, didn't you? You never told me, when all the time you knew. You probably even told him our plans for ambushing the gang when they came after the nugget, because of some stupid romantic notion about a boy who convinced you all his lies were true."

"No," Jo protested, but he kept speaking over her voice.

His jaw jutted dangerously. "I don't want to hear your explanations. You're probably making up lies anyway. Get upstairs before I decide to lock you in."

For a moment further denial trembled on Jo's lips, but the sense of rage and betrayal her uncle displayed caused it to die, unspoken.

She turned and walked up the stairs, into the room that had seemed so cozy and was now her prison.

How could she make him understand? *Would* he have understood if she'd told him everything from the beginning?

Hours later, lying sleepless in the darkness with the headache brought on by crying, Jo sat up abruptly when something struck her bedroom window.

She waited, heart pounding, and the sound came again: a small rock thrown against the glass.

She crossed the room in the blackness and peered downward, but there was no one in the pale lamplight that filtered through the downstairs curtains.

She kept her voice low. "Who's there?"

"It's me," Rufus said just as quietly, taking it for granted that she recognized his voice. "I have to talk to you. Come down and meet me out by the barn."

Mingled excitement and terror flooded through her. "I can't. I'm locked in." The judge had made good on that threat an hour or so after he'd sent her upstairs. That helped to turn some of her despair to an anger that continued to simmer.

There was a brief silence before Rufus said, "All right. Wait a minute. I'll climb up."

The latticework at the end of the porch was bare of the roses it had been planned to carry. Jo listened as he sought out hand- and footholds on it, then crept across the slanting roof.

A moment later he slid a leg over her windowsill and she moved aside to allow him to enter her darkened room.

"If my uncle finds you here he won't even give you a trial," she told him unsteadily. "He'll shoot you on the spot."

He didn't seem to hear. "Slade stole something big from that store in town," Rufus said. "I didn't see it, but they were all excited about it. I overheard some of their talk, and they're leaving the country as soon as they recover it from town where they left it hidden. You have to tell your uncle, and maybe he can get to it first."

The nugget! Rufus knew where it was! Exultation surged through her, but was quickly subdued.

It seemed unlikely that the judge would believe anything she said at this point; but she'd have to try, wouldn't she?

Jo's voice was almost normal when she said, "Tell me."

15

Rufus crouched below the opened window.

"Wait a minute," Jo said. "I'll light the lamp. That should be safe enough."

Her hands were already moving, lifting the lamp chimney, striking the match, when he said, "No, don't!"

"My uncle won't think anything of it if he notices," Jo assured him, fitting the chimney back on and adjusting the wick so that it didn't smoke before she turned to face him. "And it'll be easier . . ."

Her voice trailed off as she saw his face. He looked utterly exhausted. "What's happened?"

His voice was flat. "I figured Comanche—my horse—would head for home. Back at the farm where we used to live before Slade sold the place. But I knew I couldn't go that far on foot, and the gang's been camping out at an abandoned barn west of town that was a lot closer." A touch of defiance came into his words. "I figured they owed me a horse. No way I can get away from Muddy Wells without one, so I went looking."

Jo swallowed, waiting. His face was a mess. It made her hurt to look at it.

Rufus swallowed audibly, one hand absently rubbing the

arm that he'd injured earlier. "It was coming on dawn when I got close to the barn, but they weren't sleeping. Moss and Burbury were out by the corral behind the barn, cutting out horses, getting ready to ride. They'd caught Comanche—he whinnied when I eased up around the end of the barn—but I couldn't reach him without being seen. I could tell the gang was getting ready for something big; Burbury and Moss were excited, talking too much. They were spooking the horses some, so they milled around, and I couldn't hear all that was said. The gist of it was the gang was heading back to Muddy Wells, and they wanted to get there by a certain time. They were planning something that was going to make them all rich. Moss said, 'I'd feel better if we just took it and cleared out. I don't like the idea of going back later and taking a chance on getting caught. We should just keep it and ride out with it.' And Burbury said, 'Slade's got it all planned, and he's smart. The posse's bound to set out after us, and the townsfolk will be watchin' too. This way, when we split up, if they catch anybody, they won't find what they're looking for. Whoever's loose will be able to go back, and it'll be safer this way. Slade swore if they put any of us in jail, he'd get us out before they strung us up. One rider won't attract no attention, especially when they think the loot is already out of town, and Cleet doing his half-wit act won't be suspicious.' They both snickered then," Rufus said. "Cleet's not really a half-wit, but he's mean enough so even if he was, he'd be dangerous."

Jo's legs were unsteady, and she slid down onto the edge of the bed to hear the rest of it.

"They finally got the horses saddled, and I didn't know what to think when they saddled up Comanche too. Nobody ever rode him but me, and he'd buck like crazy if anybody tried. There was no way I could get to him then. I figured after they left, I'd take another horse. Only when Cleet and Slade showed up, they opened the corral gate and chased the rest of the horses out, swatted them on their rumps and sent them running out across the fields."

"Uncle Matthew's horses?" Jo asked in little more than a whisper.

"Some of them," Rufus admitted. "Anyway, the gang mounted up and rode off, leading Comanche and another spare mount. I tried whistling in one of the other horses—I could see them slowing down half a mile a way—but they kept on going. Didn't seem anything to do except set out walking, but it was daylight by then and those danged posters with my picture on them were liable to be anyplace. So I decided from the look of things the gang was gone for good—they didn't leave anything behind in the barn where they'd been sleeping, and why else would they run off all those good horses? I hoped they'd left something to eat, but there wasn't a mouthful. They're not planning on going back there. I didn't hear anything about where they're hiding out until they come back for their loot."

Excitement stirred within her. "But you think they'll be back to town after it?"

"That's sure what it sounded like," Rufus conceded. "I'd have come in sooner if I'd dared to move in daylight, but I was afraid everybody knew what I look like, and if they caught me, they'd string me up without giving me a chance to talk first."

Jo exhaled her held breath, thinking of trying to explain to the judge when he was so angry he'd locked her in her room.

"Where is the nugget, then?"

"A gold nugget? Is that what it is? Well, I don't know for sure, only that it's in town, somewhere close to where they stole it from, and that they're coming back after it, if they haven't already done it. Or maybe it'll be just Cleet who comes."

Jo's hopes, just raised, began to sink. If she'd been able to tell her uncle exactly where the thieves had hidden the nugget it would have been an easy matter to locate it and prove the truth of what Rufus said. But with such a vague idea of where to look, would the judge even try? Or would he assume this was a ploy to give Slade and the others a chance to get away?

"You don't have any clues as to where the nugget is, though." The disappointment was crushing.

"Only that the plan was to leave it somewhere close to the place they stole it. I doubt if they've already gotten it back; there are too many people still moving around in town. I think they'll wait until they're less likely to be seen. At least it's still in Muddy Wells, not being carried far away from here. The sheriff's maybe got a chance of catching Cleet when he comes back for it, don't you think?" His expression clearly begged her to believe that, but Jo wasn't sure she could.

Outside, lightning flashed, followed by a roll of thunder as the awaited storm broke. They both jumped, but the weather didn't hold their attention for long. Jo rubbed her hands together as if they were cold, though the heat in the room was still oppressive. Rufus got off the floor and sat on the chair beside the window.

"Will you talk to your uncle?" he asked.

Jo laughed bitterly. "Right this minute I don't think I could convince him the house was on fire if the flames were singeing his eyebrows." She flinched when the lightning came again, closely followed by another roll of thunder. "He's furious because he found out you brought back my locket, and I didn't tell him, and that I knew you were in the barn. You didn't run off his horses, though, did you?"

"No. That was the gang too, before they stole the gold. Maybe some of the horses will turn up, they were running in this direction the last time I saw them. This nugget must be a big one, the way they changed all their plans to go after it, and forgot about how valuable the horses were. I don't suppose they wanted to run far and fast with all the horses, so I knew whatever they were stealing was a lot more valuable. It's a big joke, hiding it right under the sheriff's nose."

"It's the biggest nugget I ever heard of," Jo confirmed. The excitement began to resurface. If they could find the nugget, maybe the judge would believe Rufus really wasn't part of the gang. Only where did they look?

"Are you sure they didn't say anything more about where they hid it?"

"No. Only that it was close to where they stole it, and that one man—probably Cleet—was going to come back and get it when it was safer to get it out of town. It sure didn't sound like they expected to leave it where it is for very long."

Jo bit into her lower lip. "If they're caught, they'll be put in jail. And probably ha—" She broke off, not wanting to use the word. She rose off the bed. "As soon as Uncle Matthew comes back, I'll try to tell him. Maybe he can figure out where to look. It would be better if he doesn't see you."

Rufus unconsciously began to rub his sore arm again. "If he doesn't come home soon, maybe we'll have to tell someone else," he said. "I thought if *you* talked to your uncle, maybe the judge . . ."

Jo considered quickly. "I don't know if he's the best choice. He's pretty mad at me right now, and even madder at you. No, let me think a minute."

The sounds of the storm must have covered the smaller sounds inside the house. Ordinarily the stairs creaked, and Jo would have heard anyone coming.

As it was, she heard only the click as the key turned in the lock. She turned in alarm as Rufus knocked over the chair in his haste to dive for the open window.

The judge was quicker, however. He threw open the door and moved swiftly enough to catch Rufus by one ankle as the boy plunged out onto the roof where the trellis offered a pathway to safety.

The judge was clearly furious. He dragged Rufus back into the room and slammed him against the wall. "You're a nervy wretch, I'll say that for you, but we'll see what it does for you to look at the world from behind bars. You won't be taking liberties with my house or my barn again, nor anyone else's, either!"

Jo tried to gather her wits, to think of a way to explain in such a way that there was some chance of being believed, but the judge was in no mood to listen. The first spatter of rain hit the window and blew in onto the floor, where it quickly collected into a puddle; the judge ignored it, still with his hands on both of the boy's shoulders, slamming him against the wall again and again while Jo tried to stop him.

Contemptuously, her uncle flung her aside, his nostrils flaring in anger. "I knew you were trouble the minute I saw you," he told her. "Lying, deceitful, like all the other females I ever encountered!"

Stung, in anger as well as with the pain of a bumped elbow, Jo held her ground. "Uncle Matthew, it isn't the way you think! Rufus came back to tell us that the gang hid the nugget, and they're coming back—"

"Be quiet!" the judge snapped. And then, as Jo opened her mouth for another attempt at explanation, he bellowed over her wavering words, "Do you hear me? *Be quiet!*"

"It's true, Your Honor," Rufus said desperately. "If you'd listen to us—"

His head thudded against the wall as the judge shook him one more time.

"What's going on?" Andrew had come to the doorway, his hair tousled from sleep, eyes wide. When he realized who Rufus was, his mouth sagged open.

The judge spoke without looking at the little boy. "Go downstairs, Andrew, and bring me the length of rope hanging beside my hat in the kitchen. Hurry!"

Andrew gulped, glanced at Jo for guidance and found none, then scurried away.

"Uncle Matthew, you can't do this! Rufus couldn't help anything that happened," Jo cried, grabbing his arm to try to keep her uncle from battering Rufus any further. "Can't you see his face? They beat him up, and they'll kill him if they catch him!"

The judge, however, was in no mood to be reasonable. He was obviously convinced that the boy was guilty and that Jo had conspired with him and so was guilty too.

Andrew reappeared with the rope, and Rufus, not fighting back but trying to explain, was trussed up and dragged out into the hall. For a moment Jo feared he was going to be thrown down the stairs.

"You're making a terrible mistake," Jo cried, fighting angry tears. "Please listen to Rufus, and maybe you can catch the whole gang."

The judge was breathing heavily and glared at them, but he seemed to have heard at least part of what she'd said. "I mean to catch them, but I won't be sidetracked by what this young whelp has to say. I'll turn him over to the sheriff until I get back from the trial in Dry Gulch. Then we'll have another trial here. In the meantime, the boy can tell Sheriff Dalton all the lies he wants. If Dalton believes him, he can check his story out."

He was listening, Jo thought numbly, but he wasn't hearing the meaning of what they were telling him. He didn't *want* to believe them. Anger had robbed him of reason, as Grandma had said any number of times about people who had temper tantrums. They did foolish things when they weren't getting their own way.

"Andrew, go in your room and stay there," the judge said crisply. Andrew, who had only tried to help by bringing the rope as ordered, took on a wounded look. "And you," the judge said, turning to Jo in such a way that she withdrew quickly out of his reach, "will stay put, as well. If you can't be trusted, you'll have to face the consequences."

She held her ground, however, a few feet away from him. "What are you going to do with Rufus?" she demanded.

"He'll get what he deserves," the judge said flatly. "And so will you, when I have time to deal with you." He pulled the door shut in her face, and she heard the key turn in the lock, the scrape when it was withdrawn. That meant that Andrew couldn't free her, she realized in despair.

There were bumping sounds on the stairs as Rufus, his protests futile, was guided roughly down them; then silence.

Jo's eyes burned, and helpless fury made her tremble. She wouldn't give in, though.

She went to the open window to listen. The wind and the rain would have covered anything but the loudest of sounds. I have to do something, Jo thought. But what *could* she do?

She believed Rufus. She believed the gang had hidden the nugget somewhere in town, but how long would it be there? Surely Slade planned to retrieve the gold as soon as possible, and what better time than at night, under cover of a storm during which no one would be outside to see them? Somehow she had to notify Sheriff Dalton as soon as possible. Maybe he would listen, even if the judge didn't.

Nobody would believe Rufus if they didn't get the gold back.

If Rufus were locked up in jail, he would eventually be tried for robbery and maybe even for the killing of the bank president in Dry Creek if the authorities thought he had been one of the gang members there. The result of any such trial was scarcely in doubt. There was plenty of evidence to convict the whole gang, including Rufus, and the sentence would be the usual one: hanging.

Somehow she had to clear Rufus of suspicion, and the best way to do that was to relay information from him that would lead to recovery of the nugget. Then the sheriff would believe Rufus was innocent, wouldn't he?

She remembered her uncle and how blinded he was by his own rage so that he had no understanding whatever, and Jo couldn't put down a choking fear. What if someone *did* shoot Rufus on sight, before anyone had a chance to check on his story and find out it was true? And every moment she delayed, the greater the chance that Cleet would already have retrieved the nugget.

She could see nothing outside except when the lightning flashed, and then only for a matter of seconds. After a moment, Jo blew into the lamp chimney to put out the light, then returned to the window, and after a few minutes the night seemed a little less dense.

Retracing her steps to the door, she called out in a low voice. "Andrew?"

"I didn't do anything wrong," he replied immediately from across the hall.

"I know you didn't. Neither did I, and even Rufus was forced to ride with the gang. I have to help him, Andrew."

"But Uncle Matthew locked you in," her little brother pointed out. "And he took away the key."

"Did he lock you in too?"

"No. But he told me to stay in my room." Indignation was clear in his voice.

"Did you see where he took Rufus?"

"Downstairs," Andrew said.

"But did he take him out of the house? Are they both gone?"

"I don't know."

"You've got to find out," Jo said tensely, close to the door.

"How? I'm supposed to stay in my room."

"Andrew, this is a matter of life and death! If we don't get Rufus free, they may hang him!"

After a moment's silence, Andrew asked, "What will they do to us if they catch us helping him?"

"They don't hang schoolchildren," Jo said, hoping she was telling the truth. "And Aunt Harriet's going to send for us soon. She wouldn't let them lock us up for very long. We have to try, Andrew. Sneak downstairs and see if you can find out where Rufus is."

"What'll I say if the judge catches me?"

"Make up something. Say you had to go to the outhouse."

"He'll say use the chamber pot."

"Say you're hungry. He might be angry, but he won't beat you for that." Again she hoped she was telling the truth. "It's me he's angry at, not you."

"All right," the boy said after a moment.

She didn't hear him descending the stairs, but she felt that he had gone.

She waited, then, in the dark, with nothing to do but think—about Rufus, about what might happen to him. How could her uncle be so stupid? She didn't blame him for being upset about his missing horses and the theft of the gold nugget that had been in his safekeeping even though it didn't belong to him. But how could he have looked at Rufus's face and not at least have wondered who had beaten him up, and why? Why hadn't he listened to what Rufus had to say before he decided Rufus and Jo were lying? Had cold fury robbed her uncle of all reason?

"Jo?"

The voice was small and scared, and she sprang up to return to the door. "Did you find out where Rufus is?"

"He's gone," Andrew said."

"Did you see Uncle Matthew?"

"No. I think he took Rufus to jail."

Jo wondered what to do next. Once they had Rufus behind bars, there would be no way to save him if the sheriff felt the same way the judge did.

Behind her, the flash of light that split the sky momentarily lit up the window, and the thunder made the house vibrate under her feet. She had to wait until it had subsided before she could speak to Andrew again. "See if you can find the key to this door."

"I looked on the nail where he keeps some keys," Andrew said. "It wasn't there. I think he put it in his shirt pocket."

"Then I'll have to do something else," Jo said between clenched teeth.

"What?" Andrew wanted to know.

"Rufus came up the trellis and across the roof. He would have gone back the same way. If he could do it, so can I."

She didn't wait for Andrew's response, which in any case would have been drowned out by the storm. She wished she had a pair of trousers to put on, but she did not.

"Jo? I want to go with you," Andrew said. There was a touch of panic in his voice. "I don't want to stay here alone."

"It would be safer," Jo said, and then hesitated. Could her little brother be of any help if he went with her? He had roamed around more, knew the town better than she did.

"You'll get soaking wet," she said tentatively.

There was a touch of stubbornness in his voice. "I want to go, Jo."

She made up her mind. A nine-year-old wouldn't be much protection, but at least he'd be company.

"All right. Meet me on the front porch as soon as I can get down there."

Jo heard his murmured response before it was drowned out in thunder. She crossed to the open window, felt the rain blowing in on her, and drew up her skirts into an awkward bunch around her middle.

A moment later she had swung one leg over the windowsill and was backing out onto the roof below.

16

For a moment, after the intense heat and dust of the past few days, the rain was welcome. But by the time Jo reached the edge of the roof, groping her way inch by inch and finally waiting for the lightning flashes to find her way in the blackness, she was soaking wet and beginning to feel chilled.

Panic assailed her when she couldn't locate the top of the trellis. It was definitely too far to jump to the ground. Then as the sky lit up all around her, making a fireworks display to equal that of any Fourth of July, she found the latticework, and her hand closed on one of the slats.

It didn't feel all that sturdy, and she hesitated. Rufus had climbed it, though, without pulling it loose from the end of the porch, and her only other choice would be crawling back up the sloping roof to her room to wait until the judge returned with a key.

The very thought renewed her anger against her uncle. His lack of fairness, his unwillingness to listen, made her almost hate him at that moment. So he thought all females were lying and deceitful creatures, did he? He hadn't even given her a chance. Well, she'd show him that this female, at least, wouldn't crumple and give up just because he'd gotten loud and nasty.

She felt for a foothold on the trellis and began to make her way cautiously down. Her dress was sodden, and she couldn't hold it out of the way when she needed both hands to cling to the wooden slats. She cursed the society that insisted females must wear such cumbersome and impractical garments instead of trousers, and eased her way down.

When a slat broke under her weight, Jo experienced terror, but only for a moment. She could have been no more than a few feet from the bottom, and though she fell, she wasn't really hurt.

There, she thought with a surge of triumph, I'm down. She scrambled to her feet, wet clothes molding to her body and legs. Now she was free.

Free for what, though? Lamplight spilled across the covered porch as Andrew came through the doorway, hesitating before he stepped out into the rain.

"What are we going to do?" he asked, sounding very young.

She was shivering. Whatever she did now was going to make her uncle even more furious with her than he already was. "You can stay here. That way Uncle Matthew won't be mad at you too."

"No," Andrew said, reaching for her hand. "I'd rather go with you."

"All right. Let's go," Jo said, and they set off in the wet, windy darkness.

Up there in her room, with the door locked to keep her a prisoner, she had been compelled by fury of her own, and indignation. Those emotions still filled her, but they didn't solve anything.

How she longed for her grandmother! Grandma would have known what to do next. For a moment her tears blended with the rain that continued to pelt her so heavily it stung her face. How she missed Grandma with her practical wisdom and her certainty that she could handle whatever was necessary.

Jo was not certain at all. Not of anything, except that she didn't want anything bad to happen to Rufus, who didn't deserve what this whole town would assume he deserved. Only she, of all of them, knew that he was a victim of Slade's gang just as much as the rest of them were.

Grandma had based many of her decisions on what she'd read of God's word; but even if the Good Book had been at hand for her to study, Jo doubted it would have provided her with an answer to her present plight.

The judge thought Rufus belonged in jail, to be tried with the rest of the gang when they were apprehended. The judge felt that if he were tried, the jurors would correctly determine his guilt, and that Rufus could then be punished according to the laws of Texas.

The trouble with that was that there was so much evidence against Rufus, and so little except his own word to refute it. Would they even let Jo testify on his behalf at a trial? Not if Judge Macklin had anything to say about it, she thought grimly. He'd probably keep her locked up until the trial—and the hangings—were over. And even if she were allowed to tell the jurors what she knew, would they believe her?

All of this went through her mind as she slogged through the stormy night toward Main Street, feeling Andrew's hand growing colder in her own. She wanted to do what was right, the way she'd been taught all her life to do, but what *was* it?

From the judge's point of view, it was to stay in her room and let justice take its course. She already knew she couldn't do that. It wouldn't really be justice at all.

Lightning struck somewhere ahead of them, beyond the

town, and the following thunder was deafening. She paused and put her hands over her ears as Andrew pressed his head against her body, waiting until the racket subsided. Jo stared up at the sky, lit up with an electrical display that seemed to lift the hair right off her head. For a moment she forgot the rain running off her face and her hair.

"Grandma," she said aloud, "where are you? Can you still hear me? What am I going to do? How can I save Rufus?"

There was no answer of course, only the ongoing storm and the pounding of her own heart.

After a moment she went on, head bent against the wind, tightly holding Andrew's hand, until she came to Main Street, where a few windows still showed lamplight.

From the saloon came the sounds of music, voices, laughter. The storm had not subdued the customers of the Silver Dollar. But there was no help to be found there.

The minister, perhaps? Jo wondered. If there was any spiritual guidance to be found in the Bible for such a circumstance as this, he would know. Yet she remembered last Sabbath's sermon, when in addition to preaching the gospel the man had sought to impress upon the congregation the importance of law and order. When he spoke of working with the sheriff to put an end to the indignities being perpetrated against the citizens of Muddy Wells by stage robbers and horse thieves and murderers, the man had looked deeply into the faces of his listeners, as if warning each of them to look to his own behaviors. Jo had a strong conviction that the minister would side with the other adults in this matter.

Besides, she didn't know where he lived. She wouldn't even be able to find him tonight. And after listening to the men of Muddy Wells discuss the outrages of Slade's gang, she was afraid that tomorrow might be too late. A lynch mob might storm the jail if they knew Rufus was there. They might swing a rope over the nearest tree without waiting for a trial at all.

If she didn't accomplish a rescue tonight, she might not have another chance. If the gang came back and retrieved the nugget tonight, there would be nothing to prove Rufus's sincerity and his innocence. And when her uncle discovered she had defied him and escaped from her locked room, he would take steps to assure that she had no further opportunity to do anything on the boy's behalf.

Andrew had to trot to keep up, but he didn't complain as desperation drove her along the board sidewalk, toward the jail where the judge had presumably left Rufus. Were adults always the ones who were right? Was the *law* always right? Weren't there some exceptions to the Code of the West, which demanded swift punishment for wrongdoing? What if they were mistaken about who was guilty?

There was no one to whom she could turn, as there might have been at home. The minister and the neighbors there had known her all her life, and they would have listened.

For a moment she thought of the schoolteacher, Miss Brown, but though Jo liked her, she wasn't sure of her, either. After all, the woman appeared to be smitten with the judge and might not want to take sides against him.

There was the sheriff's office. Jo stopped, having difficulty breathing. It was dark, seemingly deserted. Was Rufus in there or not? Where else might he have been taken?

Jo glanced nervously around. She wasn't sure whether she was more afraid of encountering her uncle or of having Slade and his men materialize out of the darkness behind her.

It was impossible to tell if anyone moved in the deeper darkness at either end of the street. Jo took a deep breath and tried the door. She half expected it would be locked, but it wasn't.

It was warmer, almost stuffy, inside. The place smelled of tobacco and leather and sweat. The lingering aroma of the barnyard, no doubt from the boots of men who worked with horses, made a background to all the rest.

"Rufus?" Jo spoke in a whisper, and when there was no answer, she spoke aloud. "Rufus, are you here?"

"Nobody's here," Andrew murmured.

Jo's stomach was in a knot. Surely they hadn't already executed Rufus. The judge was a stickler for legalities. Rufus was entitled to a trial, and they wouldn't have been able to do that so quickly.

Andrew pressed against her side. "Where are we going to look for the nugget?" he asked.

There was no Grandma to advise her. There was no tablet of stone handed down from on high with a ruling to fit this situation. There was only, Jo realized, her own intelligence, and her conviction that Rufus had been truthful. Slade's gang had stolen the nugget, then hidden it somewhere they thought it could be easily and safely retrieved later. They might be trying to do that right now, for all she knew.

So, then, where could it be?

She voiced her reasoning aloud. "They broke into the back door of the Mercantile and took the nugget out that way. They hit Mr. Salicky over the head and knocked him out, and they were in the alley and wanted to get away before the stampede was under control, because by then they were more likely to be caught. So what would they have done with a nugget so big it would be about all a man would want to lift or carry very far?"

"The Doane boys play in the alley all the time," Andrew

stated. "There's not much out there except dirt. Under the back steps, maybe?"

"I wish I'd brought the lantern from the barn," Jo said. "I thought we'd find somebody here."

"There's a lantern here," Andrew offered. "I saw it, on the sheriff's desk when we brought him a message from Mr. Doane. There were matches there too. Why don't we borrow it?"

A giggle that verged on hysteria rose in Jo's throat. "If we're going to steal from somebody, why not the sheriff? All right. Let's see if we can do it by feel."

A few minutes later, lighted lantern in hand, they rounded the corner into the alley.

The wind and rain pelted them with what seemed almost solid blows. Behind them, across the way, a burst of ribald laughter issued from the Silver Dollar, but the street and the alley were deserted. They ducked their heads and hurried around the building into the alley.

Even the lantern didn't help a lot, but it was better than nothing. There was no time to worry about being seen. There was only the urgency of doing something to help Rufus before it was too late.

She lowered the lantern to peer under the steps at the rear door of the Mercantile, but there was only the dirt that had turned to mud when the rain ran under the stoop. It would have been too simple, she knew, but disappointment was a bitter taste in her mouth. Where, then?

"Maybe under the Doanes' steps?" Andrew suggested. "They're only a few doors down. The seamstress's shop doesn't have any steps. They don't use their back door. This is the drugstore, and"—he splashed in a puddle that was deep enough to wet the bottoms of his trousers—"this one is the funeral parlor." A moment later he bent over, then straightened. "No, nothing there either."

"Where then?" Jo muttered in frustration. "If they carried the nugget out of the alley, seems to me they'd just have taken it with them, right out of town."

More out of despair than because she expected results, Jo reached up to lift the latch of the door to the mortuary. To her surprise, the door eased open.

"This isn't even locked!" she exclaimed.

Andrew's face was pale in the light of the lantern, his hair slicked down with the rain that dripped off his nose and chin. "No, Mr. Doane doesn't lock the back room. All he keeps here are the finished coffins, and who'd want to steal those? He locks the door into the rest of the place, though."

"Coffins?" Jo felt a chill run down her back, and something else as well. She stared at the dark crack along the edge of the door. "Are there . . . dead people in them?"

Andrew reached past her and pushed the door inward, uperturbed. "No, I told you. Just the coffins he's made up for when he needs them. There's a body in the one in the parlor, up front. The funeral is going to be tomorrow. You want to see it?"

"No! Andrew, do you think . . . might the gang have hidden the box with the nugget in it . . . in a *coffin*? Could they have gotten at them?"

"Sure. There were even some sitting right out here in the alley a couple of days ago, while he worked on them. When they were finished we helped carry them into the back room. The gang could have seen them then, if they came through the alley looking for the way into Uncle Matthew's store."

Above them lightning flashed again, and thunder drowned out whatever else Andrew was saying. Jo flinched, and when it was over, she lifted the lantern, extending it ahead of her through the doorway.

Her heart was pounding. It was silly to be afraid of empty coffins—or even one with a body in it, actually—but she couldn't help it.

"We'll have to look. If Rufus is right, they must have found a hiding place not much farther away than this."

Jo took one step through the doorway, and then dropped the lantern as a large hand came out of the darkness to close around her wrist, jerking her into the back room of the funeral parlor.

17

Terror sucked all the air out of her lungs.

Another pair of hands snatched up the lantern before the oil could run on the floor and start a fire.

"Hush! Get down, over there!" a familiar voice said, and Jo's legs turned to jelly as she allowed herself to be shoved into a corner. A moment later Andrew joined her, crouching on hands and knees.

"Uncle Matthew?" Andrew asked, and was immediately silenced by an order that brooked no argument.

The lantern was quickly extinguished, but not before Jo caught glimpses of the grim-faced men surrounding them, and the stack of wooden coffins against one wall. The judge was here, and Deputy Shaker, and the undertaker, Mr. Doane.

It was very black without the lantern, except when lightning flashed just as one of the men eased the door closed. Jo heard her own breathing, and Andrew's. For long seconds they waited, hearing no other sounds. Then Mr. Shaker said in a very low voice, "Get these young 'uns out of here."

"No time," the judge said urgently. "Somebody's coming. Don't breathe!"

Jo took the last to be directed at herself and Andrew. She

held her breath as long as she could, then let the air out silently and tried to go on breathing as noiselessly as possible.

Thunder crashed, and another electrical display silhouetted a hulking figure as the door was once more eased inward. Andrew's hand crept into hers and she squeezed it hard.

The figure entered the back room of the mortuary, and the door closed behind it. The slashing rain and the wind covered the small sounds of Jo's own breathing, but she heard the newcomer. He sounded as if he had been running.

He seemed to know his way around, for without hesitation he crossed toward the coffins. The fresh-cut pine smell of them was strong.

Jo's heart was pounding. Whoever the intruder was—Cleet?—she was glad she and Andrew weren't here alone with him.

Wood creaked and scraped and she imagined the bandit lifting the lid on the top casket and sliding it aside. She needed air and didn't dare draw it in, and her chest ached.

The rasp of a match startled her almost as much as it did the intruder, and Jo gulped aloud without thinking.

It was Cleet Slade, all right. Even in the dim glow from the lantern Mr. Doane had just lighted, Jo could tell. She hadn't seen his face when the stage was robbed, but he looked enough like his brother to convince her of his identity.

The coffin lid he was removing slid away from him, crashing to the floor, and he grabbed for the gun in the belt slung low on his hips.

"Don't do it," Deputy Shaker warned him. "You can't shoot more than one of us before the other one plugs you."

For long seconds Cleet hesitated; then he slowly allowed his hand to fall away from the six-gun. His lips drew back in a feral snarl as he looked from the judge's weapon to the deputy's, and he spat out a profane string of words.

"Mind your language, sir," Mr. Doane reprimanded. "There's a young lady and a child present."

"Relieve our guest of his weapon, Mr. Doane," Deputy Shaker suggested, and the undertaker stepped quickly to do so. Then he opened the outer door and called into the stormy night. "You can come in now, Sheriff."

A moment later the storage room seemed overfull as the sheriff and two other men, weapons drawn, joined those already assembled there.

Upon seeing the last one to enter, Jo's eyes went wide.

Rufus was as soaked as all the others, water dripping from the brim of his hat, his shirt plastered against him like a faded plaid skin. His eyes met hers, then skittered around at the others.

"Can you identify this man, son?" the sheriff asked.

Rufus swallowed, looking at the intruder. "Yes, sir. Cleet Slade."

"You prepared to testify against him in court, the way you said?" the judge asked.

"Yes, sir." Rufus sounded scared, but firm.

"Fine," the sheriff said with satisfaction. "You want to hang alone, Cleet Slade, or tell us where the rest of the gang is?"

Cleet's word was unprintable. Jo flinched from the venom in it. She could easily believe he would have beaten up a boy with those clenched fists.

Sheriff Dalton was unperturbed. "No matter. We'll get them. Maybe even yet tonight. Will they come in, do you think, to look for you, when you don't show up with the nugget?"

Cleet's gaze slid toward the lidless coffin, and the sheriff smiled. "The nugget's gone. We removed it before you got here. But of course the rest of the gang don't know that. We'll leave a reception committee in case they come here. We'll have another one waiting for them at the jail if they think to break you out. And we'll have a few good men on the road, one each side of town. We'll get your friends, don't worry about that." The smile vanished. "So why don't you save us all some trouble and more time out in the wet and the mud, and tell us which direction they'll be coming from."

Jo blanked out Cleet's cursed response. She shifted her eyes toward Rufus and found him looking at her. For long moments they stared at one another in the dim lamplight, not speaking. Then, ever so slowly, Rufus began to smile, just a little.

Jo felt herself smiling back.

The judge's curt voice cut through the room. "Well, looks like the rest of you can handle things from here on, unless you need me at one of those watch points. I don't want to send these two home by themselves, just in case any of the gang are already hanging around."

"No, Your Honor, go along. We have plenty of guns. Rufus? Why don't you go along back to the jail? You can bunk down there in the dry until we get the rest of the gang."

For an alarmed moment Jo thought they were locking him up with Cleet, until the boy said, "Thank you, sir."

It's going to be all right, Jo thought in overwhelming relief. They had finally listened to Rufus, and believed him enough to come looking for the nugget.

She didn't think to offer God her thanks until they were home, dried out, and she had gone to bed. Not even the fury of the worst storm she had ever endured could diminish her satisfaction that Rufus was no longer in danger of being hanged, though she wouldn't truly relax until Tom Slade and the others had all been captured. And that, she prayed, might even happen before morning.

The day dawned fresh and clean and sunny, only the mud and blown-down branches from the trees around the house bearing testimony to the violence of last night's storm.

Violence. Jo shivered a little as she went downstairs to find that the judge had already eaten and was preparing to leave.

The look that he gave her brought her to a halt, expecting to be assaulted by a barrage of angry words about her behavior last night.

Instead, he only said, "I'm leaving on the stage. I shouldn't be gone more than a couple of days."

She moistened her lips. "Did . . . did they catch the rest of the gang?"

"No." The curtness, Jo decided, was for that failure rather than ongoing displeasure with *her*. "I've arranged for Wister to come home with you when you close up the Mercantile tonight, so you won't be alone. And there'll be someone watching the store all the time."

They were watching when Mr. Salicky was struck down, Jo thought with an uncomfortable thickness in her chest, and when the nugget was stolen.

"Unless Andrew is with the Doane boys," the judge added, "keep him with you. Don't let him go wandering around by himself."

"You think Slade's gang might do something to him— to us?"

"He might. He's bound to be furious that the nugget got away from him. Oh, four of my horses came home."

"Good," Jo said. "What about Rufus?"

"He knows enough to look out for himself." The judge buckled on his gun belt, the leather creaking from the weight of a pair of six-guns.

"I mean, where is he? What will happen to him?"

"He's not under arrest, far as I know." The judge reached for his hat and settled it on his head.

"You did finally listen to him." Maybe she shouldn't have said that, but she felt compelled to speak.

He paused then, once more looking directly into her face. "If you hadn't made me so angry, I might have listened sooner."

Indignation flooded her. *She* had made *him* angry! Jo compressed her lips to contain her feelings; his expression warned her she'd be unwise to express them.

After a moment he moved toward the doorway and said, "While I'm gone don't go anywhere except between here and the Mercantile." Then he was gone.

Jo called Andrew, fixed him breakfast—he was easy to satisfy when it came to meals, he'd eat anything, hot or cold—and they headed for the job she seemed to have inherited for an indefinite period. She was too nervous to feel like eating bacon and eggs herself.

As they approached the Mercantile, a slim figure rose from the steps and stood waiting for them. Jo's heart quickened along with her steps.

"Rufus! Are you all right? Where did you spend the night? You're not arrested, are you?"

Rufus grinned, shoving his hat back so that the coppery hair showed. "Yes, I'm all right. I spent the night in jail, but no, I'm not arrested." He sobered. "I see your uncle didn't lock you up again."

"No. He had to leave on the stage, and he needed me to open the store." Jo twisted the key in the lock and shoved open the door, leading the way inside. "The sheriff didn't catch up with Slade and the others yet?"

Andrew had trotted off down the street to meet the Doane boys, while Rufus followed her into the Mercantile. "No. I think they're hoping the gang will try to ambush the stage."

Jo removed her bonnet and put it on the shelf under the counter. "You sound as if you don't think that's going to happen."

Rufus shrugged. "They might. They thought they had that huge nugget, and when Cleet didn't show up with it, Slade will figure either that his brother ran off with it or got caught trying to get it out of town. Either way, he'll be mad. He might try again for the nugget—anybody'd guess it would be on the first stage out of town——though he'd have to realize he couldn't take them by surprise this time. And he might try to break Cleet out of jail. I'm not sure."

Jo lifted the ledger onto the countertop, where it would be handy when the customers showed up. "It makes me feel . . . creepy . . . to know they're still loose out there."

"Me too," Rufus admitted. "Slade wouldn't want us to testify against him, so I reckon I and anybody who was on that stage when he robbed it might line up in his sights if he was to come across any of us."

Jo regarded him gravely. "Uncle Matthew said there would be guards on our house and the Mercantile. What are *you* going to do?"

"That's what I came to tell you." The grin reappeared. "I got me a job. At least for a month or so. Out to Deputy Shaker's ranch. I can bunk with the other hands. He can't pay me much, he said, but it's a place to live and he says the grub's good. After the last couple of days, any grub at all will be an improvement."

Jo smiled back at him. "That sounds wonderful."

"I'll be riding with the other hands, and they all carry six-guns, so I'm not too much afraid of Slade showing up, even if he finds out where I am. I'm going to get Comanche from Judge Macklin's corral and lead him behind Mr. Shaker's wagon out to the ranch later on this morning. I didn't want to go without saying good-bye, and thanking you for trying to help me."

Jo's face clouded. "I wasn't much help. Uncle Matthew wouldn't listen to me."

"He did, though. I mean, not when he was so angry up there in your bedroom, he didn't want to believe you, but he *heard* you. Enough so on the way dragging me to the sheriff's office he asked me some questions, and then he listened. So they figured out the nugget must have been hidden along that alley behind the buildings. Your uncle remembered Mr. Doane had been making coffins out there earlier, and they called him down to look around, and found the nugget. At least the judge was fair when he realized I was telling the truth."

It wasn't until Mrs. Hilson came in with a long grocery list, and Rufus had gone, that what he had said struck Jo. He would be living well out in the country, on an isolated ranch. She might not even see him again.

That depressed her somewhat, but all she could do was stay busy and make the best of it.

The day the judge returned from Dry Gulch, there was another letter from Aunt Harriet. The new baby was colicky, the oldest boy had chopped his foot with an ax, and the anticipated sale of the cabin had fallen through, but several other possible buyers had appeared on the horizon. They were not to worry. She would be ready to travel with crying baby and limping son by the time one of the interested gentlemen handed over the cash from the sale of the land.

Jo supposed she ought to write back to her aunt with the news from Muddy Wells, but she couldn't quite bring herself to do it yet. Not with so many things unresolved. She suspected Aunt Harriet would take a dim view of the inability of the law to round up known bank and stage robbers, especially when they were a threat to her own family.

Jo waited for her uncle's displeasure to descend upon her as soon as he came home. She wasn't sorry she'd climbed out the window, though it seemed that Rufus had talked the authorities into following the only lead any of them had, and they'd retrieved the nugget without her. But what she had done was right, she told herself.

She was prepared to defend her actions, but the judge gave her no opportunity to do so. In fact, she hardly saw him.

He was gone when she went downstairs in the morning, and since he hadn't left a key to the Mercantile, she assumed he didn't expect her to be there.

The storm had allowed the temperature to drop a few degrees, but before long it was once more scorchingly hot. In spite of the discomfort, Jo rolled up her sleeves and joined Mrs. Bacon in a thorough housecleaning. This passed two long days and left Jo so tired that she fell asleep without worrying at night.

After a while it was obvious that the judge wasn't going to mention the matter of her disobedience at all. Perhaps she should have felt relief. Instead, Jo resented the fact that none of what she felt could be brought out into the open, that she had no opportunity to express her feelings. There was certainly no apology on the part of her uncle for having refused to listen to her.

Andrew returned one day from the Doanes' with the news that a jury had been rounded up and that on the following day, since the rest of the Slade gang had apparently vanished, Cleet would go on trial by himself. The judge had not even bothered to tell me that much, Jo thought, disgruntled. She longed for the summer to be over, for it to be time to journey to meet Aunt Harriet back in the Piney Woods. Except for regret over not seeing Rufus again, she couldn't wait to leave dusty Muddy Wells forever.

Although she thought she knew what her uncle's reply would be, Jo worked up the courage to approach him after supper the evening before the trial. She had made it an especially tasty meal: thick steaks and fried potatoes and a salad made from vegetables from Mrs. Bacon's garden, besides the usual corn bread with butter melting into it. She'd also, under the house-keeper's directions, put together her first blackberry pie, and though the judge had only grunted assent when she offered him a second slice, she knew it had pleased him.

He sat at the kitchen table, working on the books from the Mercantile, while Jo washed and dried the dishes. When she hung up the towel, she cleared her throat.

"Andrew said Cleet is going to be tried tomorrow."

"That's right," said Judge Macklin without looking up.

She cleared her throat again. "Could . . . could I go to the trial?"

He did look up, then. "Expect you to testify," he stated.

She ought to have anticipated that, but she had not. "Oh. Oh, yes."

Rufus would be testifying too, no doubt. Jo's mind raced, mentally sorting through what she had to wear, choosing her best dress. And she would wear her precious locket out where he could see it.

She didn't know whether she was more thrilled or scared, to be part of a trial that might end with Cleet eventually dangling from the end of a rope.

The rest of the gang, wherever they were, knew that this would be their fate too. It would make them desperate. Had they left this part of the country forever, abandoning Cleet, or were they still out there somewhere? Waiting? Plotting a rescue or revenge?

In the warm summer evening, Jo shivered.

18

On the day of the trial Jo woke to saffron skies and an oppressive atmosphere. The air felt thick.

She gave it little thought, however, as she dressed carefully in her favorite pink dimity. She knew it was becoming. Her only regret was that it wasn't silk, such as Miss Brown wore, but Grandma had believed in practical fabrics that could be worn for everyday after they had done duty for Sunday services.

It was a little short; she'd have to let down the hem, but there was no time to do it now. She had grown since she had last worn it. She wondered if Uncle Matthew would allow her to have some of the new yard goods at the Mercantile to make herself a couple of dresses before she returned to Huntsville.

Andrew greeted her in the kitchen with the news that the judge had already gone. "We're to meet him at the Silver Dollar by nine o'clock," he said. "Do you think they'll ask me to testify too? I mean, I was on the stage when it got robbed, the same as you."

"I don't know," Jo murmured, though she doubted it. Children were not ordinarily called upon as witnesses—nor were young girls—unless there were no adults to testify. "Finish your breakfast, and don't forget to put the butter back down the well. I think it's going to get hot."

They arrived at the saloon-turned-courtroom well ahead of time. There were plenty of people ahead of them, pushing in to find seats before they were all gone. A trial was a form of entertainment as well as a gratifying end to a bandit who had preyed on honest citizens.

Mr. Doane was there, and Mrs. Hilson in her fanciest hat, ready to testify. Mr. Levinger was no longer in town. He had taken care of his business in Muddy Wells and then departed in great haste to a more civilized part of the world.

Jo took a seat near the back of the room. The tables had been pushed out of the way, and extra chairs brought in. Deputy Shaker had already brought over the prisoner, who slumped sullenly at a table near the bar. Mr. Shaker and the sheriff stood talking beside Cleet, and the sheriff kept one hand resting on the six-gun that protruded from its holster, ready for trouble if it should arise.

Jo knew the law officers had half expected an attempt to break Cleet out of jail. It hadn't happened, but they continued to be watchful.

The judge stood behind the bar, a few papers and a gavel in front of him, speaking to several men Jo thought were part of the jury. Until now this had seemed unreal, but suddenly she knew just how deadly serious it was. The sober men assembled around the two tables at the front of the room would hear the evidence and decide whether Cleet was guilty or innocent, and then Judge Macklin would pronounce sentence.

Neither the verdict nor the sentence was really in doubt.

Jo swallowed hard and looked away from these men who held the power of life or death over the man who had held up the stage and shot the driver and then stolen the huge nugget.

She couldn't bring herself to look directly at Cleet. She didn't want to think about how he must be feeling at this moment. She didn't want to have any sympathy for him.

The Doane boys had escaped their mother's attention and were giggling in a back corner. When Andrew slipped off to join them, Jo pretended not to notice. Let them enjoy one another's company if they liked.

Up front, Cleet suddenly shifted position and raised his head, drawing her unwilling attention. For a moment Jo thought he was staring at her, then realized his gaze was fixed on someone slightly behind her. She turned her head and saw that Rufus had just entered.

He was immediately aware of Cleet's ominous glare. Rufus hesitated, saw Jo, and nodded. She saw him gulp in a quick breath, and knew that he too was nervous about testifying.

Jo regretted that there was no vacant chair next to her so that Rufus could sit with her. She wasn't sure he'd have done so, anyway. Disappointment swept over her as he found a seat across the aisle, on the opposite side of the doorway.

She didn't know if it was because she was nervous, or because she'd taken time only for a glass of milk instead of her usual breakfast, or because it was rapidly growing unbearably hot in the room, but Jo suddenly felt as if she were suffocating, and she was queasy as well.

The woman next to her, a stranger, gave off an overpowering scent that was, abruptly, more than Jo could bear.

The idea of throwing up right here in court with all these people watching was alarming. Jo rose abruptly and turned to the doorway, afraid that if she didn't have some fresh air immediately she would disgrace herself.

No doubt she'd lost her seat, but she didn't care. The judge had indicated that she would not be called to testify until after everyone else had done so; she wouldn't be missed for a few minutes.

As she pushed through into the open, she heard the gavel smack sharply onto the bar, and heard her uncle calling the court into session.

Jo sucked in air and willed her stomach to settle down. It wasn't cool out here, either, but at least she wouldn't get sick from that heavy perfume. She stood on the board sidewalk, breathing deeply.

After a few minutes she thought it was working; her head felt clearer, and she no longer feared throwing up. The sky seemed even more yellowish than it had earlier; she hoped it wasn't going to storm again, though maybe that would relieve the heat for a short time.

Behind her, at the far end of Main Street, sounds caught her attention. Jo swiveled to see the eastbound stage was approaching at a sharp clip.

It slowed for a passenger to climb out, then came on along the street. Jo's curiosity was mildly aroused when she saw that there were horses tied behind the coach, but she was too absorbed in her own situation to think about it.

If she walked a short distance, made certain her stomach had settled down, then she'd go back inside and stand against the wall if there were no seats, until she was called up front. She was determined to speak firmly and audibly when her turn came, and not to tremble under Cleet's intimidating glare.

She had gone no more than thirty feet when she heard the stage team draw up behind her, and booted feet, moving swiftly, on the boardwalk.

In front of the saloon? Not before the hotel where the stage usually disgorged its passengers and unloaded its cargo? Jo slowed and turned without trying to sort it out.

She had only a glimpse of the two men disappearing into the Silver Dollar, but one thing registered all too clearly.

The men were moving fast, and each of them held a six-gun in either hand.

There was no driver up on the box. He must have been one of the men who'd just gone into the saloon-courtroom. And as Jo took a few steps farther she could see the led horses more clearly.

Her breath caught in her chest. Four horses, and she recognized them.

They were saddled, their reins looped loosely so that they could be jerked free at a moment's notice.

Inside the Silver Dollar, a shot was fired.

Without thinking, Jo began to run as she heard the shouted orders. "Everybody else stay put, or we'll shoot the lot of you!"

She recognized that voice too. Dear God, no, she thought in a panic, but there was no indication that God heard.

Jo faltered to a halt between door and stage, unable to think. The door burst open, and the first person she saw, propelled ahead of Tom Slade by a violent shove, was Rufus.

Jo had no weapon. She didn't know if she could have used it on other human beings, anyway, and she wouldn't have risked hitting Rufus in any case.

The man who had dropped off the stage earlier had obviously gone around to the back door of the saloon. Jo recognized his faded red shirt as he came through the doorway, followed by Cleet.

Two expressions were imprinted on Jo's consciousness: the stunned fear on Rufus's face, and the glee on Cleet's.

The only thing Jo could credit later for her own action was that it was divine intervention.

She certainly didn't spend any time thinking about it. She didn't weigh consequences.

She was only a few yards from the horses. She crossed the space with no recollection of moving, and brought her hand down in as hard a slap as she could manage on the nearest one's rump. At the same time she yelled as ferociously as any Apache warrior on the warpath.

The bay gelding reared, came down crashing into the mare beyond him, and stampeded them all.

Even the stage team, startled by the horses galloping past them, were urged into a run.

The next few minutes were a jumble. Men poured out of the saloon, guns drawn, and Jo was deafened by the fusillade of exchanged shots that followed.

Slade's gang had rescued Cleet from the courtroom and taken Rufus hostage (to shoot him? Jo wondered wildly), but without horses they were at a distinct disadvantage. Virtually every man in town was in the saloon, most of them armed, and they outnumbered the Slade bunch twenty or thirty to one.

When it was over, Slade himself lay bleeding on the board-walk.

The rest of the gang, though still on their feet, had suffered less serious injuries, as had a few of the townsfolk, but miraculously, there were no fatalities.

"That was sure enough quick thinking," Rufus said at her elbow, and Jo let out the breath she had been holding for so long her whole chest hurt.

This time it didn't take so long for her to remember to say a silent word of thanks.

She didn't have time to come up with another plea for mercy, however. She was about to sit down on the edge of the sidewalk and give herself a chance to recover when someone in the crowd set up a warning howl.

"Tornado coming!"

Like most Texans, Jo had seen tornadoes before. But she'd never been directly in the path of one.

The twisting black cloud came out of the saffron sky, moving so swiftly that there was little time to get out of its path. Rufus grabbed Jo's arm and pulled her down, but there was no time for anything else.

Jo pressed her face into the dirt of the street, glad for Rufus's weight helping to hold her down.

The wind came, unlike any she'd ever experienced before. Particles of dirt scoured her exposed skin, and she screwed her eyes tightly closed and wished she had something to hold on to.

With the wind came sound. The scream of it was deafening, and various unseen objects pelted her with the force of a kicking horse. She might have heard cries around her, and once she was sure she heard breaking glass as she and Rufus clung together and waited.

When they finally sat up, dazed, bleeding from small cuts, able to watch the bruises appearing on each other, Jo could scarcely believe they were alive.

Rufus was the first to gather breath for speech. "Danged if this isn't one of the most exciting days I can ever remember," he said, and amazed Jo by throwing back his head and laughing.

A few moments later, though, it was hard to feel anything but horror at what was left of Muddy Wells in the aftermath of the worst tornado the town had ever seen. Jo felt stunned as they made their way through the rubble.

Roofs had been taken off. Windows were smashed. The already pathetically few trees were mostly uprooted, even the big cottonwoods around the judge's house. The steeple remained on the church, but the bell had been carried out of it and deposited in a stock-watering tank half a mile away.

The judge had been luckier than some. There were shingles missing from the roof of the house, and the trellis intended for roses was reduced to kindling. The barn had been laid on its side but was otherwise intact. A few houses had disappeared altogether, and most others were damaged.

The Mercantile still stood, though most of the merchandise was scattered as far away as the church bell. A box of long underwear was eventually discovered, with the lid still in place, in Miss Brown's front yard in what remained of her primroses.

The townspeople gathered at the church to give thanks. No one had been killed.

"I wondered how I was going to get through this whole long summer," Jo wrote a week later to Aunt Harriet.

Now I know. Everything in Muddy Wells needs fixing or replacing, and I'm going to get to do my share of it.

I already got to help Doc Scobie put on bandages, and Rufus helped too, setting broken legs and stitching up the bad cuts. None of us got hurt very bad except bruises—I have a huge purple spot in a place I can't show anybody—and Uncle Matthew had a gash in his head that bled something awful, but it didn't stop him from regaining control of his prisoners. Because of the tornado, everybody in town has been too busy to go ahead with the trial, but they've put up the scaffolding for the hanging. Rufus says everyone will go to see it, but I won't, and I won't let Andrew go, either.

A rancher by the name of Holcomb found the stage driver about five miles out of town. The Slade gang

hadn't shot him, but they left him on foot when they stole
the stage. The whole county knew Cleet was on trial that
day, and the gang thought they'd surprise us all and
rescue him by sneaking in on the stage.

Modestly Jo refrained from explaining her own part in
obstructing that attempted rescue.

Rufus hasn't gone back out to Deputy Shaker's ranch yet.
I think Mr. Shaker just wanted to give him a place to
stay; he couldn't afford to pay him a man's wages. Now
everyone needs help, with so much damage from the
tornado. Though most of them can't pay wages, either,
they're giving Rufus room and board to work fixing
things. He's going to be here for the next week, replacing
our lost shingles.

Here Jo had paused for a moment, smiling. She had
figured out what she was going to cook while Rufus was here,
sharing Andrew's room across the hall from her own.

The sheriff got back a little bit of what the gang had
stolen when they robbed the stage, but they'd already done
something with most of it. Mr. Levinger didn't stay long
enough to get any of his two hundred dollars back. He
had to telegraph to Boston for money to go home on, and
Andrew said he seemed very glad to be leaving Muddy
Wells behind. Someday I hope I can see Boston and find
out if it's really so much better than Texas. Miss Brown
says she doesn't think they have gully washers like the one

we had, that turned all the streets to mud and washed away everything near the creek that wasn't fastened down. And heaven only knows what he would have thought of the tornado. Miss Brown's chicken coop was carried away, but Andrew has promised to build her another one. I hope he can do it. Maybe Rufus will help him. I like Miss Brown.

We had a good rain after the tornado, except for the fact that so many people were missing their roofs. The little creek behind the house is full, and we waded in it.

Jo paused to chew on the end of her pen before she dipped it once more into the inkwell.

Muddy Wells hasn't been too bad, for a short time. Certainly some exciting things happen here. But we miss the Piney Woods and long to return home.

Uncle Matthew still calls me "girl" instead of by my name. He never did apologize for being so unreasonable, but he lets me do the books for the Mercantile, so I guess he trusts me now. Men are rather peculiar, aren't they? They complain a lot, and they don't always listen to what you say. But there's something rather interesting about them, and when you need protection, or something done, they seem quite capable most of the time.

I look forward to meeting you at the end of the summer, and seeing all our friends and neighbors in Huntsville.

Sincerely, your obedient niece, Josephine Eleanor Elizabeth Whitman.

She reread that last part, then crossed out "obedient." She was in the process of folding it for mailing when she was struck by another thought. She added a postscript.

I've just had a brilliant idea. You said you would be needing some help to expand Grandma's house, and I know just the person. By the time we're ready to go home, all the repair work will be done in town. Rufus grew up on a farm and he knows how to do everything. He can plow fields, milk cows, mend fences, and use a hammer and saw. I'm sure he'll be just the one to help you add on to Grandma's house and do the heavy work. I'm going to ask Uncle Matthew if he won't pay Rufus's passage on the stage too. After all, if it hadn't been for Rufus we might not have gotten the nugget back, and that would have been most embarassing for the judge. So he owes Rufus something, don't you think?

Again she folded the letter, and again she was struck by additional thoughts. She unfolded the paper one more time and added a final postscript.

I remember what beautiful antimacassars you used to make for wedding presents. Mama loved the ones you gave her for our best chairs. I suggest that you start some new ones, because I think eventually there is going to be a wedding here. Miss Brown has set her cap for Uncle Matthew, I believe. So far he hasn't weakened, but she's very clever and quite pretty. She asked if she could sit with us in church last Sabbath, and he just grunted and slid over to make room for her. I think he's beginning to soften a bit.

I can't really think why Miss Brown would have chosen Uncle Matthew when there are other single men in Muddy Wells who have better dispositions. But Grandma always said a good woman could bring out the best in a man if there was anything good there in the first place. Perhaps Miss Brown sees something in the judge that the rest of us can't see. It's too bad we probably won't be here for the wedding, if there is one.

This time she folded the paper all the way and put the cork back in the inkwell. Then she got up from the desk and went outside to see how Rufus was doing with the dam he was helping Andrew build across the creek, before the water was gone and Muddy Wells reverted to being all dry and dusty again.